THE WELL

Compiled by

Rebecca Xibalba and Tim Greaves

Illustrations by John Sinclaire-Thomas

The Well

Copyright © 2021 Rebecca Xibalba and Tim Greaves
TimBex Productions

CONTENTS

THE WELL

Tim Greaves

In the heart of Surrey there exists a sizeable area of land known as Blechnum Woods. Almost 1200 acres of unsullied beauty, a rare surviving example of what so much of England used to look like before widespread deforestation schemes left their ugly, irreparable mark.

Within those woods, a myriad of ancient trees – believed by some to be more than a thousand years old – stand watch like silent, aged sentinels, protecting their home from the remorseless ravages of mankind.

Almost exactly in the centre of Blechnum Woods, in a small, natural clearing, there stands a beautiful stone-built well. How old it is nobody knows. It is a relic of a time long past, a time before records and title deeds and land registrations existed, and by extension records of changes to and erections upon that land.

Local folk from Blechnum and Egsa-Aston – the two villages which bookend the woods – will attest to the fact that the well and the clearing in which it sits have scarcely changed. Not in their lifetimes at least.

Octogenarians who have lived there all their lives, recalling how they frolicked in the woods as children, will swear to you that the well looks exactly the same today as it did 70 years ago. Whereas this might seem highly improbable and it's much more likely that someone has tended it over the years – just as one might cut back the overgrown foliage from the grave of a loved one, perhaps – nobody has ever come forward to admit that they are responsible for doing so. Yet, if you were to visit it today, you would see for yourself. Except for the vast swirls of ivy that have worked their way into the ancient mortar of the clearing's centrepiece, there it sits in that timeless, enchanting space, as unblemished as the day it was built.

Some believe it must have been used to provide water for a village long since gone and forgotten. Although there is no documentation to support this thinking, it's a reasonable enough conclusion to draw. Others with more fanciful ideas will claim that it has connections with royal blood. This too is unproven.

There are one or two people in both Blechnum and Egsa-Aston, however, who will tell you in hushed tones that the well represents something far more sinister; that it harbours an evil history, and a distinctly sordid one at that.

This is where things become particularly intriguing, for a little research proves that what those people say is true.

The early part of the 17th century was a dark period indeed, particularly so for womankind. As the instigator of the Original Sin – and thus often perceived as allies of the Devil – many women lived a fearful existence. It was little wonder that they would seek and cleave unto a husband, for only within the sanctity of marriage might they find any hope of safety from the accusations that ran rife among small communities.

For the unwed it was a different matter. All but the most God-fearing in a village could be singled out as dissolute and find herself indicted of witchcraft. It made no difference whether she was innocent or guilty

3

of the accusations levelled against her. There were no exceptions for those accused of sorcery, and whatever form the ensuing trials may take, the woman would always be the victim.

Some were forced to flee for their lives before their persecutors were able to deal with them. Many perished in the wilderness; others were simply never seen again.

Once targeted, those who refused to run in the foolhardy belief that their innocence would be proven endured the most terrifying of ordeals at the hands the pious, self-righteous elders, some of whom were in truth more depraved than the casualties of their cruel deeds.

Hypocrisy was rife and nowhere was transgression more flagrant than among those who deigned to pass judgement in the name of God. Members of the Clergy would extract confession from even the most virtuous of women and by all manner of hideous torture, not only physical but mental too. They would take perverse delight in coercing their victims into revealing the most intimate details of their sexuality, stripping them first of their dignity and then, in the wake of all manner of inconceivable humiliation, their lives.

A noteworthy case of the hypocrisy which plagued England at that time can be found in the private journals of Reverend Hugo Bartholomew, rector in the village of Blechnum from 1617 to 1669 and practicing witchfinder.

A venerated member of the community, it was only after Bartholomew's death in 1673 that his diaries were found and evidence came to light revealing another side to his persona. By night he would seek out the prettiest, most poverty-stricken girls in the village. Having lured one in with the promise of riches which would never be delivered, he would subject them to his vile, prurient desires, then seal their lips with the threat that if they spoke out about what had passed between them he would see them drowned as witches in the well at the heart of Blechnum Woods.

Fear was a very effective silencer, but it was never enough for Bartholomew. Every single one of the poor women detailed so luridly in the pages of his journals was subsequently documented as having been tried for practicing witchcraft, dragged to the well and drowned.

According to Bartholomew's journals, only one woman ever chose to challenge him. She paid the price dearly.

Born in 1621, Bethany Woolacott was one of history's most powerful, not to mention youngest acolytes of the Black Arts. She was also among the first known practitioners of breaching, a ritual by which a long needle would be used to puncture the skin of a willing disciple. Bethany would then eagerly consume the blood during spell-casting. The parallels with vampirism speak for themselves.

Among her many disciples were dignitaries of the Church, for Bethany believed that coercing sacrilege within the priesthood was essential in order for her spells to work. The Reverend Hugo Bartholomew never conspired with Bethany personally, but he knew only too well of priests from neighbouring environs who did. And although he was well aware of Bethany's practices, since her father was one of the wealthier residents of Blechnum he chose to turn a blind eye.

Double the corruption.

Instead, Bartholomew focussed his attention upon innocents, whom he would drown for their crimes against God; crimes they never committed.

Then one night in 1640, Linette Woolacott, Bethany's younger sister fell, prey to Bartholomew's carnal desires. He later wrote that he knew not who she was, and since those journals were private, there is no reason to suspect he wasn't genuinely alarmed when he discovered his faux pas. But the damage was done. Linette Woolacott was just 15 years old when the Reverend Hugo Bartholomew raped her.

A week later, no longer able to keep her silence, Linette broke down and revealed to Bethany what Bartholomew had subjected her to, Later that day, after evening prayers, Bethany confronted the man in his own pulpit, swearing that he would pay for what he'd done to her little sister.

Painted into a corner, the next day Bartholomew had Bethany arrested under accusations of witchcraft, and following a short trial condemned her to death. Her father did nothing to intervene.

If you should choose to look into it, you can find the archaic texts in the original Latin script, presented during the verdict of death passed upon Bethany Woolacott:

Surrey. Juratorespro dno Rege psentant qd Bethany
Woolacott, nup de Blechnum in com pdco, spinster, existens
cois fascinatrix et incanatrix, deum pre oculis usis non hens, sed
instigacone diabolica seduct vicesimo octavo die Septembris
1640 Blechnum pd in com pd felonice suscepit vpp vnam
calvam extra innominatus sepulchrum.

The translation of this text reads as follows:

Surrey. The Jurors for the lord the King so present Bethany Woolacott, late of Blechnum in the county aforesaid, spinster, being a common witch and enchantress, not having God before her eyes, seduced by the Devil's will on the 8th September in Blechnum to feloniously receive a skull drawn from an unnamed tomb.

It's hard to believe that this fictitious, trumped up charge could ever have held water, nor that it could result in an execution. But it did.

What happened to Bethany in the days following her arrest is open to speculation; it is something of which there is no record. But the methods used by witchfinders to extract confession were merciless. Girls would have needles forced into them. If their pain threshold was higher than that deemed to be normal then they would be decreed unnaturally insensitive and therefore guilty. Razor cuts would be inflicted upon the most private and delicate parts of their bodies. If they didn't bleed as freely as it was considered they should, the Devil must be protecting them and once again they were found guilty. Even a woman's size could be used to penalise her. She would be placed on scales and if it was decided that her weight was disproportionate to her height? Guilty.

On the fourth day following her arrest, Bethany Woolacott was taken to the clearing at the heart of Blechnum Woods, where she was hog-tied and lowered into the well. Her protestations echoed up from the darkness as she swore out eternal revenge, not only against charlatan envoys of God, but to all those who dared believe that some great power beyond their understanding could provide them with absolution for their misdeeds or sanction their dreams.

Bethany Woolacott had indeed been guilty of witchcraft. She was possibly the only one of the Reverend Hugo Bartholomew's victims who was. Yet she had been tried and convicted by a man not only morally corrupt but one who can only be likened to the embodiment of evil.

As the decades passed, the use of the well for nefarious purposes ceased. Yet the residue of Bethany Woolacott's final oath hung over the villages of Blechnum and Egsa-Aston like a foul reminder of their insidious past and, superstitious or not, locals familiar with its history would seldom venture into the woods, at least not without good reason and never in the dark.

For backpackers and walkers who stumbled across that clearing in Blechnum Woods it was another matter. Much as so many dreamers might – you or I included, for are we all not dreamers at heart? – when finding themselves in such an idyllic little spot and faced with such a whimsical opportunity, passers-by would toss a coin into the well as a benefaction towards the granting of a wish.

Hundreds must have passed by the well over the years and how many of those wishes ever came to pass one cannot be sure.

What we do know is that for six people things didn't go at all as they had anticipated...

BROBDINGNAGIAN
(The Growing Pains of Daisy Denton)

Rebecca Xibalba

POP!

Caron Denton jumped and almost dropped her glass of wine.

'Now look what you've done,' she screeched, turning to her little daughter Daisy, who was stood staring dumbfounded at the tattered rubber remnants attached to the piece of string in her tiny hands.

The child looked up at her mother, tears welling in her pale blue eyes. Caron pulled a tissue from her handbag and fruitlessly dabbed at her cream-coloured dress, which was now decorated with a cherry red stain. 'Honestly child, one of these days!...' Caron seethed through gritted teeth, trying to hide her anger from the other guests at the party.

'I'm sorry, Mummy,' Daisy whimpered, her head hung low.

'Just get out of my sight,' Caron hissed.

Daisy slunk away, dropping the busted balloon into a rubbish bag as she passed.

She looked around the room, awash with a sea of legs and feet. A jumbled hum of voices resonated in the air above her and she felt very small and insignificant. She *was* small, just a smidge over a metre tall, about average for a five-year-old, but sometimes she felt a hell of a lot smaller. Not tiny or anything silly like Thumbelina or The Borrowers, but with no brothers or sisters – and no friends due to the fact she was home-schooled – Daisy lived in a world full of giants and it often left her feeling *very* small indeed.

She spotted a brown cube-shaped beanbag on the far side of the room beside the patio doors and weaved in and out of the adults towards it. Without her balloon she suddenly felt very vulnerable, and the leather pouffe looked like an appealing place to sit, safely out of the way of the throng of giants. As she flopped onto the beanbag, the middle slumped and the sides rose up around her like a big hand. This feels lovely, she mused; nice and cosy.

Scanning the huge kitchen, Daisy's eyes darted from one side of the room to the other. Her attention was drawn to a large, red-faced man in the middle of the room who had just let out a deep, bellowing laugh. Now he *was* a giant, well over six-feet tall and wider than the average doorway. Daisy giggled, for he reminded her of the Fat Controller from one of her favourite books.

It had been raining all day, which was why the party was being held indoors. Madison Hughes-Larkin and her husband, Jason, were expecting their third child. The promise of a beautiful sunny afternoon in August had been ruined, perhaps as a cruel joke on the part of Mother Nature who, at the mention of a baby shower, decided to treat them to just that: a shower. This soon turned into a downpour that had dashed any hope of the alfresco gathering in honour of the impending arrival of Hughes-Larkin junior the third. The worst of it was clearing now though and the last traces of the rain ran idly down the double glass doors, slowly being dried by the hot sun as it made its way through the clouds.

Daisy looked out into the massive garden and her eyes widened as they fell upon the large, blue trampoline in the middle of the lawn. She looked back at the party. Everyone was busy chattering amongst themselves, wrapped up in their own little world of reminiscing and idle gossip.

Dasiy hopped down from the beanbag and stepped over towards the latch on the sliding door. She looked down at her feet and her bright white frilly socks beamed back up at her. She winced. Her mother would be so cross if she went out into the garden without her shoes. But her shoes were in the hallway at the front of the house, which meant she would have to get through all those people again.

She put her index finger into her mouth and thought hard. After a moment a smile crossed her face as an idea popped into her head. Of course, it was simple. Mummy was always so angry if Daisy got her socks dirty, so she would take them off. Then they would stay clean and Mummy would stay calm. She stood on one leg and yanked off her sock. Swapping to the other leg, she swiftly pulled off the second one, tossed the two of them onto the beanbag and reached up for the handle. It was just within reach, but too high for her to actually take hold of the lever and pull it down. She stood on tiptoe. Her tiny fingers hooked around the latch, but she had neither the strength nor balance to release it. She sighed as she wobbled back onto her flat feet.

A shadow cast over her and she looked up to see the jovial, rotund man had silently stepped up behind her.

14

'Are you trying to go out?' he asked in a deep baritone voice.

Daisy nodded forlornly.

The man reached over, flicked open the latch and pulled the door slightly open, leaving a gap just wide enough for Daisy to slide through.

'Thank you,' she chirped as she ran outside towards the trampoline.

The man smiled as he watched her and his nose wrinkled. 'Aww, cute,' he said quietly to himself.

'Brian!' a voice rang out behind him.

He raised a hand and waved. 'Coming,' he replied with a sigh, and he made his way back over to his impatient wife, who was waiting for a top-up.

Outside, Daisy stood beside the trampoline. The top of her head was just parallel with the rim. It was a good 14-feet in diameter and although there was a small puddle in the middle she wasn't perturbed; this looked like so much fun and she just *had* to have a go. She reached up with both her hands and pulled up as hard as she could. Managing to swing one leg up, she hooked the side of the trampoline with her foot and with all her might hoisted herself up onto it.

She looked at the puddle of collected rainwater and considered her next move carefully. Then, looking back towards the house, without another second's thought she bent her knees and slowly started to jump. She giggled as the puddle bounced up and down in the middle and ripples of water made their way across the canvas. She started to bounce harder, waving her arms like wings as she levitated from the sprung surface. The water was spreading further and, as she landed, her feet almost slipped. 'Oops,' she cried and moved a little closer to the edge, away from the puddle.

As Daisy resumed jumping she was unaware that a face was peering out at her through the patio doors. It was Madison Hughes-Larkin.

'Er, who's that on the trampoline?' Madison asked, her voice tinged with concern. But her words were lost amid the cacophony of chatter. She raised her voice slightly higher. 'Who's child is on the trampoline? The safety netting isn't on!' she exclaimed.

Caron heard and rushed towards the patio doors. All the other children were at school, so it *had* to be Daisy. Her eyes widened as she saw her tiny daughter bouncing up and down on the giant trampoline. She slid the doors open wide and yelled. 'Daisy! Get down from there!'

Daisy's head spun around to face the house and as she landed on the surface of the trampoline she lost her footing and the rebound sent her sideways, up into the air and over the side.

It possibly seven or eight feet down from her elevated position to the grass and the descent would have taken no more than a few seconds, but Daisy's mother and the assembled audience behind the glass doors watched in horror as the small child in her pretty, pink frilly dress plummeted to the ground in excruciating slow motion.

Caron put both her hands to her face. 'Oh my God!' she screamed.

A man pushed past her and rushed out into the garden. 'Somebody call an ambulance!' he yelled over his shoulder. As he reached Daisy, he dropped to his knees beside the apparently lifeless child, who was laying face down on the grass. He felt for her hand, ran his fingers along her arm and pressed on her wrist.

As his thumb and forefinger made contact with her wrist, Daisy groaned breathlessly. 'Ouch!'

She began to stir and the man moved aside as she slowly turned over. Her dress was covered in grass stains and her hair was stuck to her face. The man stared at her in surprise as she beamed a big, wide smile and said, 'Hey, Daddy. That was fun.'

Ollie Denton doted on his little girl and the relief he felt at that moment was beyond comprehension. 'Daisy, what were you thinking sweetheart? You could have been killed!'

Daisy sat up and looked down at her grass-stained dress. 'Oops,' she whispered.

Ollie reached over to her and she moved forward into her father's arms. He hugged her gently. She looked over his shoulder to see her mother approaching at an alarming pace. 'Uh-oh,' she said softly.

Ollie turned his head just as Caron ground to a halt beside him. 'It's alright darling, Daisy is unharmed.'

'*Unharmed*?!' Caron exclaimed. 'Well, lucky for her!'

Daisy looked up at her mother sheepishly and stepped away from her father's embrace.

Caron glared at her daughter. 'What the hell do you think were you playing at? You could have broken your neck,' she continued angrily.

'I'm sorry, Mummy, I just…'

'I don't want to hear it! Get inside. We're going home. You've embarrassed me enough for one day!'

Ollie stood up. 'Now come on love, there's no need for that, she's just a child.'

Caron spun on her heels. 'I'm going home, so unless you want to walk I suggest you follow me.'

Ollie looked down at poor little Daisy and held out his hand. 'Come on, pumpkin, let's get you home.'

As the Dentons made their way back through the house the other guests steeped aside to let them through.

A young, blonde-haired woman grabbed Ollie by the arm and mouthed, 'Are you okay?'

He nodded and continued out into the hallway with Daisy in tow. Her face black as thunder, Caron was coming downstairs, pulling on her jacket. She threw Ollie's at him and yanked open the front door. She almost bumped into a paramedic who had his arm outstretched to ring the bell.

Caron pushed past him and stormed off towards their car.

Ollie stopped on the doorstep, 'Caron, love, don't you think we should get her checked over?'

Caron didn't reply. There was a high-pitched double beeping sound as she opened the driver's side door and climbed into the family's SUV. The engine roared into life.

Casting the paramedic an apologetic look, Ollie hurried over to the car with Daisy hot on his heels.

Tucked up in bed later that evening, Daisy whined as her father rolled down the blind. 'It's still light, Daddy. Can't I stay up one more hour?'

Ollie smiled and sat down on the edge of the bed to give her a kiss. 'It's 7:30 and that's when all good girls should be tucked in and fast asleep, isn't it?'

'But Daddy...' she persisted.

'No, pumpkin. You gave your Mummy and me a real scare today. I think it might be good for you to lay here and think about what could have happened.'

'It was just a tampaleen,' Daisy implored through a gappy grin.

'Yes, but a *trampoline* for children much bigger than you,' Ollie said emphatically. 'You've got plenty of time to play on trampolines and things like that, but not while you're so small.' With that, he stood up and walked across the room. 'Night night, sweetheart'. He turned off the light and slowly closed the door.

Ollie descended the stairs and stood for a moment at the closed door to the living room. He wrapped his hand around the cold, brass doorknob and was about to turn it when he felt the silent pulsing of his mobile phone in his pocket.

He stepped back and walked through into the kitchen. As he withdrew the phone from his pocket, he turned it to see the screen lit up with the name "Dave (Work)" flashing at him. He crossed the room and tapped Accept with his thumb, reaching out to open the back door with his other hand. 'Hey,' he said quietly, closing the door to the garden behind him.

'Hey babe. I've been worried about you. How's Daisy?'

Ollie turned and glanced back towards the house. Satisfied his wife wasn't snooping about, he replied. 'Yeah, I'm fine. Daisy's fine too, I've just put her to bed. Gave me a serious fright though.'

'Yeah I bet,' the voice replied. 'I so wanted to give you a hug at Maddie's party, but…'

Ollie cut her off. 'Yeah I know. I'm fine though, sweetheart. Honest.'

'You know how much I love you,' she implored. 'I wish…'

Ollie was nervously keeping an eye on the back door. He interjected again. 'I know. I wish that too, you know I do. *So* much. If only wishes came true. But they don't – and we can't. Not yet.'

A light came on in the kitchen.

'Listen, I've got to go,' Ollie said anxiously. 'I love you,' he added and quickly ended the call. He rummaged in his other pocket and pulled out his VAPE just as the back door swung open.

'What you doing out there?' Caron bawled.

'Just having a puff,' Ollie replied, holding the VAPE aloft.

Without another word, Caron closed the door. A huge plume of vapour filled the air above Ollie's head as he let out a massive sigh of relief.

He returned to the house and closed the back door quietly behind him. 'Would you like a cup of coffee?' he called out. There was no reply, so he walked out into the hall. Finding the living room door closed he decided to leave the coffee and have an early night instead.

As he put one foot on the bottom stair a shrill voice called out from the living room: 'I'll have a latte.'

Ollie rolled his eyes and forlornly returned to the kitchen. As the coffee machine dripped away, he pulled out his mobile phone. He opened his messages and a little smile appeared in the corner of his mouth as he scrolled through.

'Have you made that coffee yet?'

The voice made him jump and he almost dropped his mobile phone. Slipping it back into his pocket, he turned to face his wife. 'Yes, darling, it's just ready.' He held out the mug to her and she took it without a word of thanks and stomped off back into the living room.

Ollie inserted another pod into the machine and sighed as he watched the sticky liquid drip slowly into the mug and the second pipe descended to add the milk.

He switched off the machine and walked out of the kitchen. As he reached the doorway to the living room, Caron's voice boomed out, 'Light!'

Ollie walked slowly backwards and flicked off the kitchen light.

Early the next morning Ollie couldn't wait to leave the house. The atmosphere had been extremely frosty and an attempt to warm things up had been shunned when Caron threw his arm off her and wriggled as close to the edge of their kingside bed as she could without falling out.

He jumped into the car and sped off up the road towards his job in town.

Caron was awoken by the roar of the engine on the drive. Grimacing for no apparent reason, she climbed out of bed and made her way to the bathroom. As she passed Daisy's bedroom she drummed her fingers on the door. 'Come on, Daisy. Time to get up!'

In actual fact Daisy was already awake. She pulled the colourful duvet covered in pictures of unicorns over her head.

A few minutes passed and the bedroom door opened.

'Come on. Up!'

Daisy groaned and swung her feet out from under the covers.

Caron turned and walked out. 'Get dressed, wash your face and brush your teeth. And no dillydallying!'

As her mother disappeared off down the stairs, Daisy put her thumbs to her ears, waggled her fingers and poked out her tongue.

When Daisy got downstairs, Caron was sitting at the kitchen table, eating toast and reading a tabloid newspaper.

The little girl took her place at the table, her feet hanging a few inches above the tiled floor, and reached for the box of Crispi cereal. She looked around the table for the milk, but it wasn't there. She looked towards her mother, who was absorbed in the newspaper.

'Mummy,' Daisy said apprehensively. 'There's no milk.'

Caron put the paper down flat on the table and glared at her. 'It's in the fridge, lazybones,' she said, then lifted the paper back up and carried on reading.

Daisy looked over towards the large, American-style fridge-freezer, then back at her mother, who was once again hidden behind the pages. She slunk off her chair on to the floor and walked over to the fridge-freezer. She stretched up and as the door opened wide she could see the milk on the top shelf, but she wasn't able to reach it. Exasperated, she turned back to her mother. 'Mummy. I... I can't reach, it's too high,' she whimpered.

Caron growled under her breath and slammed the paper down. She got up and marched over to the fridge, took out the bottle of milk and threw the door shut. 'There!' she declared, thrusting the plastic bottle into

Daisy's tiny hands. 'Now hurry up and eat. Your lessons start in precisely 23 minutes!'

Daisy resignedly returned to the table and ate her breakfast in silence. No sooner had she scooped up the last mouthful than her mother grabbed the bowl and put it in the dishwasher. 'Spoon,' she said impatiently, holding out her hand. Daisy jumped down from her chair and handed her mother the spoon. Then she dolefully padded off into the spare downstairs room that had been converted into a home office and took her position at the desk.

Caron strode in behind her and reached for a book from the shelf. She put it down in front of Daisy, pulled a sheet of paper from a tray beside the computer and handed it to her daughter. Daisy looked at the title on the book: **BASIC MATHEMATICS**. She sighed inwardly; she detested maths. Grabbing hold of a pen she looked up at her mother.

'Don't sit there looking at me, you know *exactly* where we left off!'

Daisy opened the book. 'Times tables?'

'Yes. Times tables. Up to 7 today please. I'll give you 20 minutes.'

With that, Caron left the room.

Daisy stared at the book for a moment. It was colourful and fun, with each set of numbers accompanied by various fruits. She took up the pen and with her tongue darting in and out of her mouth she eagerly started to solve the sums.

In less than ten minutes she had completed the task. She hopped off the chair, grabbed the paper and gleefully skipped out to find her mother.

Caron was in the kitchen, a large glass of gin in her hand.

'I've done it!' Daisy declared proudly.

Startled, Caron spun round. 'What have I told you about sneaking up on me? I'm a bag of nerves when you're around!'

'But I'm done,' Daisy protested.

Caron looked up at the clock. 'You *can't* be done. It's only been eleven minutes. Go back and do it properly!'

'But Muuuummy, I *am* done. Look.' Daisy extended her arm and flapped the sheet of paper.

Caron snatched it from her. Her beady eyes darted across the page. As she surveyed the neatly presented work, each sum answered correctly, her mouth actually dropped open for an instant. Then she scowled at her daughter. 'I suppose you think you're clever do you? I suppose you think you're *really* big?' she hissed.

Daisy frowned and indignantly answered back. 'I wish I *was* big then I wouldn't have to be here with *you*,' she snapped.

Caron was incensed. 'Go to your room you insolent little brat!' She tore the sheet of sums in two tossing the pieces into the air.

Daisy ran upstairs and the house shook as she slammed her bedroom door.

Ollie stood by the photocopier waiting for the last of his paperwork to feed through.

When he had studied architecture at university he had dreamt about vast glass buildings and unique projects that would earn him the coveted Pritzker prize. But in reality, projects like the one he was working on at present – the Meadowbridge Affordable Housing project – were his most common assignments.

As the photocopier clattered to a stop, he gathered up the pages and slipped them into a plastic wallet.

'I could have done that for you, sir.' The bright, chirpy voice echoed along the granite tiled corridor.

Ollie looked up and a broad smile stretched across his face. 'Hey there. You're fifteen minutes too late!' He looked around the office behind him and then down the corridor. Satisfied no one was about, he gave the pretty woman a peck on the cheek. She responded by grabbing his face with both hands and locking lips with him passionately.

Ollie pulled away from her. 'Candy! What are you doing?' he exclaimed.

'*You* later... if you're lucky!' She grinned and ran her tongue across her top lip. 'See you later, Mr Denton.' She turned away and her heels clicked as she sauntered off along the corridor, purposefully exaggerating the swaying motion of her hips for his benefit.

Ollie composed himself just as he heard the loud, familiar voice of Brian, his manager, echoing along the corridor.

'Good morning, Candice,' the big man boomed as he passed Candy.

'Morning, sir,' she replied politely.

As Brian approached, Ollie became aware of a significant rucking in his trouser area. Horrified, he hastily placed the plastic folder of paperwork in front of his crotch.

'Ah, Oliver. I'm glad I ran into you. How are we getting on with that awful housing estate project?'

'Pretty much done, sir. The plans have been approved. I've just reviewed the sustainability paperwork and made copies for the relevant departments, and pending the green light from the clearance company we're pretty much good to go.'

'Excellent work, son. Well done. You can take an early dart if you like, pop off home to that lovely wife and daughter of yours.' Patting Ollie on the back, Brian waddled off back in the direction from which he'd come.

Ollie pulled out his phone and opened his messages. Quickly typing with both thumbs, he sent a text and slipped it back into his pocket.

The swelling in his trousers was starting to get uncomfortable so he breathed in and thought for a moment. An early dart, back home to Caron... He shuddered. That did the trick.

Feeling lighter than air, he hurried off and took the stairs two at a time down to the reception and out into the car park. Pipping the remote to unlock the car, he opened the back door and put the folder on the seat.

Then he climbed into the driver's seat, blew into his hands to check his breath and glanced at his reflection in the rear view mirror. As he did so he saw Candice approaching. She opened the passenger side door and climbed in.

'Let's go see our little housing project in the woods shall we?' Ollie gave her a cheeky grin.

'Ooh yes, let's,' Candice replied with an equal hint of devilment.

Daisy was laying on her bed. As she sobbed, she looked over towards her favourite chocolate coloured teddy bear. 'It's not fair,' she whimpered. 'Why does Mummy hate me so much?'

The bear stared back at her blankly.

'Well, I'm not staying here. I'm running away to a place far, far away where she will never, *ever* find me!' she declared.

She reached for the bear and sat him on the edge of the bed so that he could watch her as she gathered up little trinkets and stuffed them into a small rucksack. She grabbed a little plastic shop till from the shelf and pressed the button at the bottom, releasing the drawer. She turned it upside down and shook the small plastic coins out onto the rug. Scooping them up, she put them in her pocket, slung the rucksack onto her shoulders and, grabbing the teddy by his arm, she quietly opened the bedroom door.

Dasiy stood at the top of the stairs and listened. She could hear the familiar theme tune of her mother's favourite chat show; assured that she would be glued to the television in the living room, Daisy slowly snuck downstairs. She silently crept past the living room and picked up her shoes from the rack in the hall, before tiptoeing across the kitchen floor and out into the back garden.

She sat on the step, quickly put on her shoes and then took off fast, running out of the back garden and along a narrow alleyway that led out into the large playing field that adjoined the junior school.

She held the teddy up in front of her. 'Look, Coco. That's where we're going – to the woods. They'll *never* find us there!'

She ran as fast as her little legs could carry her. In the distance the school bell was ringing and Daisy knew that the children would soon be released out into the playing field for their lunch break. Determined not to get caught, she thrust herself forward and ran at top speed towards the tree line. When she reached the far side of the playing field she stopped. Panting hard, she looked up and down in a mild panic. Brambles and nettles covered the way into the woods.

She could hear the distant sound of excited voices as the school children filtered out into the schoolyard. Making a decision, she ran along the hedges towards the bottom of the hill where old Farmer Brown lived. Noticing a gap in the brambles, she quickly stepped through. But as she made her way into the dense woodland everything seemed to get a whole lot darker.

There was a sound of crunching gravel as the blue SUV arrived at a secluded spot at the end of Waterhouse Lane.

Manoeuvring the vehicle off the track to park up beside an old oak tree, Ollie applied the handbrake and leant over to kiss his secretary. She moved towards him and thrust her hand between his legs. Ollie kissed her hard. Abruptly the seatbelt jammed and he laughed; he was stuck, suspended across the gear stick and handbrake. He released the belt as Candice gestured towards the back of the car.

They hopped out and quickly climbed back in through the rear doors. In a blurred frenzy, clothes were whipped off and Candice's foot pushed the folder of paperwork to the floor.

Daisy was starting to feel scared. She had never ventured this far from home on her own before and the shadows cast by the trees looked like hands reaching out to grab her.

'Don't be scared, Coco, it's okay,' she said timidly, with a faltering reassurance aimed more at herself than the stuffed toy. She carefully trod over the thick fallen branches and pushed on through the never-ending network of trees and bushes. Ahead of her was a perfectly straight pathway created by two lines of ancient redwood trees. She turned around to look how far she'd come, but everything just looked the same and there was no sign of the nettles or the gap in the brambles where she'd entered the woodland. She turned around again. And again. And soon she'd completely lost sense of which way she had come from and which way she was going.

She began to feel really scared. And cold. She held her beloved bear close. 'Maybe Mummy's right,' she whispered. 'I'm not so big and clever.'

A sudden beam of sunlight illuminated her and she raised her hand to shield her eyes. As she squinted, she could see a clearing up ahead, a really bright spot just beyond the trees. She smiled and ran towards it.

As she reached the clearing, she stopped. 'Wow!' she exclaimed.

Right in front of her was a well; an old stone-built round base with a tiled roof covered in ivy.

'Look, Coco, a wishing well!'

Daisy had a lot of books and several of them featured wishing wells, so there was no doubt in her mind that this is what it was. She skipped over and placed Coco on the rim. Pulling herself up, she peered over the edge. 'Wow!' she exclaimed again, and her words echoed back up at her. 'Shall we make a wish?' she asked the bear. Coco's cold plastic eyes shimmered in the sunlight. 'Yeah,' she said. 'Let's. Now, we need some silver money. I read that in my book.' Daisy felt in her pocket and pulled out the plastic coins. 'I guess this will do,' she said. She threw the handful of play money into the well and looked at the teddy bear. Shaking her head, she thought for a moment. Then, at the top of her voice she yelled, 'I wish I was big!'

31

A thick black cloud appeared and covered the sun. The small glade was suddenly plunged into darkness. Daisy went to grab Coco, but in her haste she knocked him off the edge and he plunged down into the well. With a cry of anguish, she tried to look for him over the ledge but all she could see was blackness; *everything* was black.

Frightened, Daisy sat with her back against the well and pulled her knees up under her chin. But then as quickly as it had appeared, the cloud suddenly dispersed.

Daisy stood up and promptly let out a little yelp. 'Ouch!' She rubbed the top of her head and turned to see she had bumped it on the roof of the well. She looked down. It seemed to be a lot smaller than she had first thought. How had that happened, she wondered?

With a sudden urge to get away from this place, and maybe go back home for fishfingers and crinkle chips, Daisy stepped away from the well and strode back towards the woods.

As she walked, she felt a burst of confidence course through her.

The trees didn't seem so tall and scary now, and as the fallen branches snapped beneath her feet she rejoiced in the sound of the splintering wood.

As she reached the corridor of redwood trees she stopped at the sound of giggling from somewhere over to her left.

She could see over the mass of brambles and noticed a blue car similar to the one belonging to her parents.

The giggling intensified.

Curious, Daisy walked towards the car. Stepping over the bushes she stopped and stared. It *was* her parent's car. But how could that be? It was *so* small!

The giggling suddenly ceased as a dark shadow fell over the occupants of the vehicle.

Daisy heard a small voice say, 'Someone's out there!' Then the tinted rear window slowly opened and Ollie Denton gingerly poked his head out. All he could see was a huge pair of pink trainers, and as his eyes followed the grey leggings up high into the sky he gasped to see the face staring inquisitively down at him.

'Hello, Daddy!'

ACCEPTANCE

Tim Greaves

Acceptance. A fundamental need of humankind. Such a simple thing, yet for so many people something that isn't easy to find; to be loved for who or what you are, without need to compromise in order to "fit in".

For Finlay Fortescue the innate need for acceptance had been a lifelong uphill battle. There were times when not fitting in hadn't bothered him at all, for he wasn't by any stretch of the imagination a mixer. But at other times the sadness of it was all encompassing and it crushed him.

Finlay had been obese for as long as he could remember. In fact, babyhood photographs from a time of which he had no recollection bore out the facts: he had left the womb substantially larger than the average newborn.

The thought of his mother struggling to push him out into the world crossed his mind from time to time and it amused him greatly. Sylvia Fortescue had been a loathsome woman, a domineering, unsympathetic disciplinarian and, in Finlay's opinion, an all round bad mother. Of course he accepted that being a single parent must have been tough, but did that excuse the horrible things she had subjected him to over the years? And don't forget his name, the damning product of Sylvia's perverse sense of humour and penchant for alliteration.

The day that she died had been one of the most celebratory in Finlay's life, although if he'd had any say in the matter it would have been a far more torturous departure from the world than simply passing away in her sleep; falling from the station platform and being hit by the morning train perhaps, or a sublimely glacial demise, trapped in the walk-in freezer at the butchers where she had been employed for the last eight years of her working life.

Finlay's weight belied explanation. Sylvia had been as thin as the proverbial beanpole. It wasn't as if he overindulged or ate unhealthily either, but during his formative years he'd piled on the pounds at a phenomenal rate. On the day he started school at the age of five he had weighed just a shade under 11-stone. There followed an equal number of years of living hell.

In almost every school classroom there's that slightly odd kid that the others single out for derision. Once identified by the leaders of the pack, even the shy and the introverted who'd rather disappear into the background join in the tease, more often than not as an act of self-preservation to avoid being picked on themselves.

Blubber Boy. That was the first of many names attributed to Finlay Fortescue by his classmates, and not the worst of them by a long chalk. Fat-Face-Forty; FST (which stood for Forty-Stone-Forty – 'Here comes FST!' they would cry, too lazy to even say the words); Finlay Fart-in-the-queue. Yes indeed, Sylvia's alliterative cruelty paid daily dividends for the bullies, their every jibe as hurtful as a sharp slap in the face.

Being a redhead simply provided Finlay's tormentors with bonus grenades. One of the books his primary school teacher had read to the class was Roald

Dahl's *The BFG*. Thereafter, among many other names, Finlay had become known as The BFG; not, as in the story, the Big Friendly Giant, rather The Big Fat Ginge.

Over time Finlay learned to appear nonchalant, but try as he might his eyes always failed to disguise the all-consuming hurt.

When on occasion the merriment at his expense became excessively raucous, the presiding teacher might intervene, but through the stinging tears Finlay had often detected the trace of a smirk. And what chance did he have if even his teachers saw him as a figure to be mocked? Weren't they there to look after their pupils' best interests?

He was 17-stone when he left school and, suffice to say, he had never once looked back with that rose-tinted view which people often adopt whilst mewling about the happiest days of their lives. For Finlay they had been among the worst.

He had worked his way through a series of menial jobs, at all of which he was mercilessly ribbed about his size by his colleagues; occasionally in spite, though more often in fun, but at the end of the day what's the difference? It all hurts, doesn't it?

Having been treated so badly over the years, Finlay had become painfully withdrawn, but quickly discovered that solitude suited him grandly and it became his close companion. Whilst out walking – his favourite pastime and only concession to exercise – he would sometimes see couples walking hand in hand

and wonder to himself what that feeling of propinquity might be like.

Yet as far as Finlay was concerned, women might as well come from another planet for all he knew about them. And it wasn't that he had no interest. Quite the contrary in fact. He was familiar with their bodies – masturbatory fantasies over well-thumbed magazines had been his education in that respect – but of their minds he knew nothing. They were a complete mystery to him, and he rather expected it would remain that way.

Until the day he met Rachel Appleton.

Finlay was a self-taught, self-employed computer and IT problem solver. Twice a year, every year, as regular as clockwork, he would close up his business for a week and take himself off on a little holiday.

He couldn't stand the coast. If it wasn't the infuriating cacophony of ravenous gulls disturbing the peace, it was spoilt by unruly children with parents incapable of – or, in Finlay's unwavering opinion, bluntly disinterested in – the actual job of parenting. Additionally, rather than being invigorating, there was something about the smell of the ocean that made him feel queasy.

So instead he would make a beeline for the countryside, take a room at a little B&B and go for long walks. Despite the 37-stone in weight that he carried around with him, he would be out all day and ramble for miles, relishing the tranquility and the solitude.

And so it was that at the age of 47, one day late in July, he was strolling contentedly through Blechnum Woods in Surrey, unaware that it would be the morning that changed his life.

Finlay was the last person in the world to believe in the silly childhood notion that one could make a wish and have it come true. It was utter balderdash. He was only too well aware that one had to toil hard in order to get what one wanted from life.

Yet when he stumbled upon the fabled Blechnum Well on that clement Thursday morning… well, he would later reflect on that moment and swear that the ancient structure had been calling to him.

He pulled out a handkerchief and mopped his brow. Opening the knapsack slung across his shoulder he withdrew a large bottle of spring water, took several big gulps and then returned it to the bag.

Belching quietly – even when no-one else was around he considered it rude – he leant forward, moved aside some of the tangled ivy that engulfed the ledge and peered down into the hole. After only a few feet the moss-strewn stonework disappeared into inky blackness.

'Hello!' he called out, delighting at the sound of the echo that repeated several times before falling silent.

He was about to turn away when he stopped, felt in his trouser pocket and pulled out a handful of small change. His fat fingers picked through the pile of coppers and silver until he found a 10-pence piece.

He smiled at the thought of a shriveled-up, hobbit-esque goblin, lurking deep down in the darkness at the bottom of the well, snatching up the offensively stingy offerings of passers-by and resolutely refusing to grant their wishes.

Better not be a cheapskate, he decided. He selected a grubby pound coin, then immediately switched it in favour of a shiny, almost new one; if he was going to sacrifice a pound needlessly, it might as well be one that would put him in the best standing for wish approval.

Finlay returned the rest of the change to his pocket.

Now, what to wish for?

Materialistic things were frivolous and inconsequential, so it would have to be something he would benefit from for always. He wasn't a greedy man, but he had worked hard and Fortescue's IT Solutions had made him more than enough money to live comfortably. His home – an unassuming little cottage on the outskirts of Godalming – wasn't a palace, but he was as happy there as he was likely to be anywhere. Flash cars certainly held no appeal – and even if they did, he could afford one effortlessly. No, it had to be something money couldn't buy.

Unlike when he was young and would have given anything to change the situation, Finlay was no longer unhappy with either his weight or how he appeared to others. If he had been he might have wished for something like a toned, muscular physique. But that was a farcical notion, he knew he would look ridiculous, and if there was one thing he'd learned over time it was that people's intolerance of him – for whatever reason – was *their* problem, not his. Although he would still welcome a less judgemental attitude from those around him, he was now quite content being just who he was.

So what should his wish be then?

His thoughts drifted back to the cafeteria in the village where he had stopped for coffee the previous afternoon, and the young couple sitting in the corner booth, holding hands across the table, lost in each other's eyes.

Acceptance. Yes, that was it. What more could anyone ask for out of life? He might be happy in his own skin, but to be accepted and loved by someone other than his mother – and he doubted even she had ever *really* loved him – would make his life complete.

Glancing around to make sure that there was no-one about, he said aloud, 'I wish I could meet a woman who wanted me for what I am.'

As he tossed the pound coin into the well, the air suddenly felt warm and his nostrils filled with the sweet scent of Rowan.

Finlay stood still for a moment and listened. The woodland around him had fallen silent. A few seconds passed and then all at once the ambient sound of chittering birds and branches rustling in the soft breeze returned.

He shivered and suddenly felt very self-conscious about what he'd just done. Looking about him, he was pleased to see that there was still no-one else around. 'There goes a pound I'll not see again,' he chuckled. Tutting at his own silliness, he turned and walked away.

Finlay wouldn't have given either the well or his wish another thought were it not for something that happened over breakfast at the B&B the following day, although the connection didn't occur to him until later on.

'Are you staying here long?'

Startled, Finlay looked up from his plate of bacon and scrambled eggs. He had been alone in the dining room for fifteen minutes and hadn't heard the woman enter.

'Oh!' he exclaimed. 'You gave me a bit of a start.'

The woman was standing beside the window. With the sunlight glaring into his eyes through the glass behind her, Finlay couldn't see her face clearly. He raised a hand to shield his eyes against the brightness. Silhouetted by the sunlight, the woman's head and shoulders were outlined with a delicate glow. She stared at Finlay without responding.

He suddenly realised she had asked him a question. 'Oh, yes,' he muttered, setting down his knife and fork and dabbing at the corner of his mouth with a napkin. 'I mean no. I've been here for a few days already. Heading home tomorrow.'

The woman took a step forward. 'I arrived late last night. I'm leaving tomorrow too.'

As she moved completely away from the window, Finlay was able to see her face. Her complexion was like alabaster and he was delighted to see that, like himself, she too had flaming red hair, perhaps even a little brighter than his own. It hung loose to the bottom of her pale neck. She was wearing a summery white Bardot top and Finlay noticed that her face, neck and shoulders were dappled with tiny freckles. He put down the napkin, stood up and extended his hand. 'Finlay Fortescue,' he said. 'But please, call me Fin.'

The woman was a good 8-inches shorter than Finlay. As she reached out and accepted his hand her full lips formed into a pretty smile. 'Rachel Appleton.'

At the touch of her fingers Finlay felt a little flutter of butterflies in his tummy.

'As you can see I've already started...' – he gestured as his plate of food – '...but may I invite you to have a spot of breakfast with me?'

'I don't eat breakfast.' The tone smacked of impatience, as if Finlay was supposed to have known. Which was patently ridiculous. 'I don't have anything at all in the morning. I can't stomach it.'

Finlay didn't really know how to respond to that. There was an uncomfortable moment of silence, but then – possibly detecting his awkwardness – the woman spoke again, her voice softening. 'I'd be delighted to share your company while you eat though. If you don't mind.'

Finlay smiled. 'Of course not. Please, take a seat.'

The table at which he was sat had chairs for four, but instead of doing what most people in that situation would do and taking the one opposite, Rachel settled herself on the seat to his right.

'Are you sure you wouldn't like a cup of tea? Nothing like it for settling your stomach.'

'No, I'm fine thank you.'

'Of course, you know what's best for you.' Finlay positioned his generous posterior back onto his chair, shifted a little to get comfortable and resumed eating.

They made small talk for several minutes about nothing in particular whilst Finlay demolished his bacon and eggs and washed them down with the last of his mug of tea.

Just as he'd finished, Mrs Crompton, the B&B's landlady, popped her head around the door. 'Did you enjoy your breakfast, Mr Fortesque?'

'It was delicious, Mrs Crompton.'

She smiled. 'Those eggs come from a farm just up the way from here. Tom Brown – lovely man – he's been supplying me with them for years. Nothing else quite like them. Can I get you any more tea?'

Finlay held up his mug and the elderly woman stepped over and took it from him. 'Hot and wet with two sugars, please.' Finlay grinned. He looked at Rachel. 'Are you sure you won't have one? Just half a cup?'

'No, really, I'm fine.'

Neither Finlay nor Rachel noticed, but as Mrs Crompton left the room she gave them a funny look.

They sat chatting and almost half an hour drifted past. Finlay learned that Rachel was 26-years-old and a primary school teacher – he withheld his thoughts on the callousness of the educational system in his experience – and lived near Hythe in Kent. She had recently separated from her partner and had come away for a few days to get her head straight.

By the time his second mug of tea had arrived and been eagerly consumed, Finlay was ready to pop the question that had been rattling around in his mind for the past ten minutes. 'I don't wish to appear too forward, but I wonder if you would do me the very great honour of accompanying me on my walk today?'

He saw the look on Rachel's face and immediately regretted having asked. She opened her mouth to speak, but not wanting to put her in the position of having to make an excuse, he quickly made one for her, 'I'm so sorry, that was dreadfully unthinking of me. I'm sure you have other plans. You came away to be on your own.' Realising he was blathering, he paused, took a breath, and cleared his throat. 'What I mean to say is, please forget I asked.'

Rachel was looking at him with amusement. 'Do you make a habit out of inviting someone out and then withdrawing it again before they have time to answer?'

'No, of course not, I er…'

She reached out and put a finger to his lips. 'I'd love to.'

Finlay felt himself blushing. 'Excuse me?'

She dropped her hand down and as her cool fingers brushed across his own he felt his stomach do a little somersault of pleasure.

'I said I'd love to.'

Finlay's face broke into a beaming smile. 'Really? Oh, well, that's splendid then. *Really* splendid. Is there anywhere in particular you'd like to go? I have my car and we could…'

'No preference.' She removed her hand from his. 'Wherever you want to go is fine with me.'

Finlay stood up and glanced at his watch. 'Well, I must get ready then. Shall we meet at the front in about 20-minutes?'

Rachel got up. 'Make it 15,' she said, and leaning forward she planted a light kiss on his cheek. If the over-familiarity of the moment made Finlay uncomfortable, he didn't show it and it swiftly passed as she looked up into his eyes and said, 'Then I'll be all yours.'

All yours. Those words played on a loop in Finlay's head whilst he changed into something less rumpled than he'd have worn had he been venturing out alone. All yours.

Ten minutes later he was standing outside the B&B looking very pleased with himself. He was just making sure that his shirt was properly tucked in when Rachel appeared through the open door, skipped schoolgirlishly down the short flight of steps and gave him another peck on the cheek. 'Come on then, take me somewhere nice.'

Finlay grinned. 'Your chariot awaits.'

They crossed the road to where his lime green Skoda Citigo was neatly parked beside the curb. Oblivious to the twitch of the curtain in the downstairs window of the B&B, he held open the passenger door and Rachel climbed in.

Mrs Crompton watched them drive away. 'Nowt as queer as folk,' she muttered and let the curtain drop back into place.

After stopping in the village to pick up a few nibbles – sausage rolls, some bags of crisps, a Jamaica ginger cake and a couple of bottles of fizzy drink – Finlay drove out to the far side of Blechnum Woods and parked up.

They spent a remarkably pleasant morning rambling through the trees and exploring the twisty-turny little lanes that bisected the woodland at regular intervals. As they walked, they talked – about everything and nothing – and by the time Finlay's stomach began to cry out for some sustenance, they had learned they had a lot in common and it felt as if they'd known each other forever.

Settling himself on the huge trunk of a fallen tree, Finlay pulled out some of the goodies from his knapsack and set them down in the leaves. 'Help yourself.'

Rachel shook her head as she sat down near him on the trunk. 'I'm not hungry at the moment.'

Finlay frowned. 'But you didn't have any breakfast. Surely you must be feeling a little peckish.'

'I don't usually eat a lot during the day. I'll have something later.'

Finlay looked a little awkward. Then he said, 'Okay, I'll wait too then.' He started to scoop the food back into his knapsack.

'No, don't be silly, you go ahead and eat.' Rachel smiled.

'Well, if you're sure you don't mind then, I must confess I'm famished.'

'Of course not.'

Finlay broke open the package of sausage rolls and devoured one of them in three swift bites. 'Very tasty.' Brushing away the little flakes of pastry from the corner of his mouth, as he pulled out another he turned his head and saw that Rachel was staring at him blankly. 'What?' he said. 'Have I got crumbs on my chin?'

'No.'

She's looking at me the same way everyone else does, Finlay thought. She's aghast at the disgusting blob filling his face. 'I think I'll save this till later,' he said, tucking the sausage roll back into the packet.

'Wait,' Rachel said. She was smiling again. 'You *have* got a crumb. It's on your cheek.' Before Finlay could brush it away, she shimmied her bottom along the trunk, came so close to him that their hips were almost touching, then leaned in and flicked out her tongue, licking away the flake of pastry.

'Thank you,' Finlay muttered, unable to disguise his embarrassment.

He packed away the comestibles in the knapsack and held out a hand to assist Rachel to her feet.

She laughed. Such a pretty laugh. 'How gentlemanly you are, Fin.'

Hearing her say his name stimulated that little butterfly flutter inside.

'You're very welcome, Rachel. And may I add what a delightful name that is.'

'It's not my real name,' she said, brushing the dirt and loose twigs from her skirt 'Well, it *is*. But I changed it by deed poll.'

Finlay smiled. 'What was it before?'

'Promise you won't laugh?'

'Of course I won't laugh.'

'April.'

Finlay smiled at her warmly. 'What's wrong with April? It's a lovely name.'

Rachel frowned at him. 'You're kidding me. April Appleton? It's an awful name. God knows what my parents were thinking. Alliteration gone crazy.'

'I must confess, having one myself I don't care too much for alliterative names,' Finlay said. 'It gives nasty people too much ammunition. I've been called some terribly unkind things in my life.'

Rachel nodded. 'You know what the kids at school used to call me? Ape. "Here comes the Ape." Looking back it's silly how much that used to hurt – but they knew it and they were relentless.'

Hearing her say that broke Finlay's heart. 'Children can be so cruel,' he said.

A faraway look appeared in her eyes. 'Adults can too. Shall we walk?'

The afternoon passed very much like the morning and by the time they got back to the car they were holding hands. It would be fair to say that Finlay felt as if he was floating on air.

The fifteen-minute drive back to the B&B passed in virtual silence. Not uncomfortably so, rather in contentment; they had said everything there was to say for now, and both of them were happy for the opportunity to gather their thoughts. Finlay had no idea what was going on in Rachel's head, but speaking for himself he couldn't recall a day in his life that he had enjoyed more.

When they got back to the house, Finlay walked round, opened the passenger door and helped Rachel out.

'Always the gentleman,' Rachel said.

Holding hands, they crossed the road and went inside.

Pausing at the bottom of the stairs, Finlay asked, 'Would you like to have dinner with me this evening?'

Rachel smiled. 'It would be a pleasure. I'm quite hungry after all that walking. You'll have to give me time to clean up and get changed though.' She stood on tiptoe and gave him a little peck on the lips. 'See you back down here in an hour.' With that she hurried off up the stairs ahead of him.

As Finlay put his foot on the bottom step, the grandfather clock at the end of the hall chimed six.

The door to his left opened and Mrs Crompton appeared. 'Good evening, Mr Fortescue. All ready for your dinner?'

'Ah, Mrs Crompton. Would it be a huge inconvenience to have it at seven tonight?'

From the expression on her face, Finlay gathered that it *was* an inconvenience, but the woman merely nodded her assent. As she turned to go back into the parlour, he added, 'Oh, and Miss Appleton will be joining me this evening, so if you could see your way clear to opening a bottle of wine that would be most appreciated. White, I think, if you have it.'

Before Mrs Crompton could reply, Finlay turned on his heels and set off up the stairs. She frowned after him. 'Who on earth is Miss Appleton?' she muttered.

Fifteen minutes later Finlay had just stepped out of the shower when there came a light tapping sound on his door. 'One moment.' Muttering under his breath, he wrapped a robe around his corpulent form and opened the door. He was surprised to see Rachel standing there, dressed exactly as she had been when they parted company. Before he could say anything, she put a finger to his lips and slipped past him into the room.

Finlay closed the door and turned to face her. He chuckled nervously. 'I'm not sure Mrs Crompton would approve of guests being in the same room,' he said jovially. He noticed that Rachel wasn't smiling. In fact she looked rather upset. 'You haven't changed for dinner. Is everything alright?'

'I wanted to speak to you about something.'

'Very well.' Finlay looked at her uncertainly.

'It's a little bit embarrassing.'

Finlay gestured to the bed. 'It's fine. Sit down and take your time.'

Rachel perched herself on the edge of the bed and looked up at him. 'Come sit beside me.' She patted the duvet.

Finlay could feel himself blushing again and he suddenly felt exposed. He pulled the robe around himself a little tighter. 'I'm not sure it would be appropriate. I'm not dressed properly.'

Rachel smiled at him coyly. 'You're not shy are you, Fin?' She patted the bed again. 'Come on, there's nothing to be nervous about.'

Making sure to leave a couple of feet of space between them, Finlay moved over to the bed and sat down. The mattress gave way beneath his bulk and the springs cried out in protest. 'So what's the matter?' he said, trying to sound calmer than he felt.

She took a small breath. 'I lied to you about something.'

Finlay suddenly felt very foolish. Here he was, sitting half-naked beside a woman he barely knew but had fast become fond of, and he'd got carried away with it all and been naïve enough to hope the feeling might be reciprocal. Now she was going to reveal that he was the butt of some cruel deception. He silently cursed himself.

'I didn't come here because I'd split up with my partner.'

'Okay,' Finlay said slowly, wondering where this was leading.

Rachel shuffled over, closing the gap between them. 'The truth is I've never had a partner,' she continued. 'I'm a bit... well, picky when it comes to men.'

With each passing moment Finlay was feeling more and more confused.

'The fact is, I have a... a thing for large men.'

'Oh!' Finlay hadn't expected that. 'I see. Well, I...'

'And I know I've only known you for a day, but I think...' She trailed off and put a hand across her eyes. 'God, I can't believe I'm saying this. I think you might be the one.'

'The one?' Finlay's mind was racing. He knew exactly what she meant, but he could hardly believe what he was hearing. This had to be a joke. His robe had come loose and suddenly he felt Rachel's cool fingers move across his thigh. He glanced down.

'Yes. *The* one.'

As Finlay raised his head again to look at her, Rachel leant towards him and kissed him hard on the lips. Before he could react, her tongue was inside his mouth and curling around his own. He had no idea what he was doing – he had never kissed a woman in his life before – but he succumbed to the moment and responded by instinct.

He broke away, gasping for breath. 'This is all happening so fast. I think...'

Again Rachel pressed a finger to his lips. '*Don't* think. Just follow your heart.' Her other hand snaked across his thigh and nudged its way down to his groin, gently parting the copious folds of plump flesh, and then those oh *so* cool fingers danced lightly across his scrotum and closed around his penis.

Immediately Finlay felt himself swell and begin to get hard. 'I don't think we ought to be doing this,' he said, but even as the words left his mouth he knew that they were going to.

Leaving him seated – his robe wide open, revealing his vast naked form – Rachel stood up and stepped away from the bed. She pulled the Bardot top over her head to reveal small, unfettered, upturned breasts tipped with pale areolas and perfectly centred nipples in an evident state of arousal.

Finlay let out a little gasp. Rachel dropped her skirt and his eyes widened as he saw that she was wearing no underpants. In stark contrast to that freckled, alabaster skin, her swollen vulva was vivid pink and there was no pubic hair.

Finlay couldn't hold back any longer. He was fearful of the response he might get, but he nevertheless felt compelled to ask the question. He gestured to himself. 'You can't really be attracted to *this*,' he said, feeling his face burning with shame.

Rachel took a pace towards him. 'But I am. You're beautiful.'

Finlay felt the tears well in his eyes. He swallowed hard. 'So are you,' he said. He looked down at his manhood, which was poking out from between his fleshy thighs, now fully erect. 'I've never…' he began. 'I've never been with a woman before.'

Rachel put a soft finger to his lips and gently pushed him down until he was flat on his back. Straddling him, she carefully lowered her crotch to meet his and he felt himself engulfed by her warm wetness. She threw back her head and, gasping with ecstasy, began to move slowly up and down.

The sensation was like nothing Finlay had ever imagined and, unable to control himself, less than a minute passed before he ejaculated into her. 'I'm so sorry,' he said breathlessly. 'I didn't mean to…'

Rachel put a finger to his lips again, climbed off and lay down alongside him.

He stared up at the swirls cut into the plaster on the ceiling. 'You're going to laugh at me now,' he said. 'But I came across a wishing well yesterday.'

'You did?' Rachel nuzzled her face into the folds of his neck. 'What did you wish for?'

'Someone like you.'

She laughed. Such a pretty laugh. And yet not quite the same as the one he'd got used to throughout the course of the day. There was something different about it, but Finlay couldn't quite put his finger on what.

'Well you know what they say,' Rachel whispered. 'Be careful what you wish for.' She nuzzled in even closer.

Finlay sighed. 'You know, if I believed this was anything more than coincidence, I'd say it was a pound well spent. My wish came true and I got exactly what I wanted.'

'Did you though?'

Finlay could feel her hot breath beside his ear. He moved away a little and turned his head to face her. 'What do you mean?'

'Get what you wanted.' Her face was blank, the same expression he'd seen briefly earlier that day, only now the eyes were staring at him vacantly and he saw that there were no pupils, just black orbs.

'I... I don't understand,' he stuttered.

It was Rachel's turn to sigh. 'I like you, Fin, I really do. So I wanted to do something nice for you before... Well, I'm sorry. I'm *truly* sorry.'

Finlay frowned. 'Sorry? What for?'

Suddenly Rachel made a little snarling sound and her full lips peeled back to reveal twin rows of yellowed teeth that tapered down to sharp points. Before Finlay could comprehend what he was seeing, her head jerked forward and with one bite she tore a chunk of flesh from his neck.

His face filled with a mixture of surprise and anguish as a welter of crimson fountained out of the gaping hole. Crying out, he feverishly clutched at his neck, feeling the warmth of his lifeblood seeping out through his fingers. He struggled to roll onto his side, but Rachel was already up and straddling him again, an immense weight that he hadn't noticed the first time now pinning him to the bed. Her mouth was coated with his blood, which was dribbling down her chin and dripping onto her breasts.

As Finlay looked up at her in disbelief he saw her upper abdomen swell and there was a hideous cracking sound as her ribs shifted and rearranged themselves, almost doubling her girth.

'But…' Finlay gurgled. 'I only wanted to be accepted for what I am.'

'And I *do*,' Rachel said. The voice wasn't even female any more. Her jaw clicked and appeared to unhinge, stretching wider and wider to reveal row after row of rotting, but terrifyingly sharp denticles. 'I honestly do accept you for what you are.' She bent down and brought her face to within inches of his. 'Food,' she whispered.

It would have only been fair that Finlay's death be swift and painless. After all, he'd not hurt another soul in his entire life. Indeed, he didn't have a bad bone in his body. But the more refined anthropophagus takes unbridled gastronomic pleasure in consuming its meal warm – and very much alive.

Yes, it was true. Her victim didn't have a bad bone in his body. But Rachel hadn't fed for almost a month and she was very hungry indeed.

Within ten minutes all that remained of poor Finlay Fortescue *was* his bones.

They say you should be careful what you wish for. Perhaps that clichéd idiom should be appended with the words "…and be careful *how* you wish for it."

58

DON'T COUNT
YOUR CHICKENS

Rebecca Xibalba

'Mornin' Tom,' a voice rang out.

Thomas Brown turned and, shielding his eyes from the bright morning sunshine, he squinted as he peered to see who had spoken. 'Ah, good mornin' to ya, Sammy lad. How's life treatin' ya these days?'

Sam hurried over and heartily shook Tom's hand. 'I'm good mate, really good. Just popped back to the village to see my parents. It's becoming a weekly ritual these days. How are *you* doing?'

Tom looked down at his shoes. He let out a big sigh and slapped Sam warmly across the top of his arm. 'Mustn't grumble, son, mustn't grumble.'

Sam pointed towards the wicker basket that Tom was swinging slowly back and forth. 'Still peddling eggs I see,' he said with an affectionate smile.

'Yes. It's all I know lad. It's all I know.'

Sam took Tom's hand again and shook it strongly. 'Well, I must go. I'm heading back home to London and don't want to miss the train. You take care of yourself, mate. It was lovely to see you!'

Tom watched the young man walk briskly off towards the station. He closed his eyes momentarily and recalled that day back in the late 1980s when little Sammy and his friends had broken into his barn and let loose all the horses. Later that afternoon Sammy's father, the village mechanic, had marched him back to Tom's farm and ordered him to apologise. Sammy had been frightened and clearly repentant, and as a form of punishment he was ordered to help out on the farm after school and at weekends for the rest of the month.

During that time Tom had become quite fond of little Sammy and his help around the farm had proven invaluable. Tom had no children of his own and having lost his wife a few years prior he had been struggling to keep on top of everything.

Tom opened his eyes to find Sam had disappeared from sight. He sighed and, turning back towards the dusty track up to his farm, he continued the short journey home.

When he reached the gates he stopped and frowned. Several hens were in the field adjacent to his land. The ramshackle fence separating them from the open space beside his farm was laying flat between two wooden posts, one of which was leaning and almost touching the ground. Tom had intended to get the fence repaired, but funds were tight and his run-down home and dilapidated farm had far more pressing issues.

He opened the gate and entered the farm. Gingerly stepping over the fallen fence, he ambled over towards the hens. As they saw him approaching they started to move away. Agitated and clucking in unison, they headed further from the fence.

In a feeble attempt to keep up with them, Tom waved his arms, desperately trying to usher them back towards the farm. As if realising they were getting further and further away from the sanctity of their coop and the rest of the flock, the hens u-turned and ran back. Deftly hopping over the flattened fence wire, they continued running until they settled back with the flock.

Tom chuckled to himself and turned to follow them. He stepped over the fence and bent down to lift the fallen post, wincing as the muscles in his lower back went into spasm.

He straightened the post and leant down on it, applying his whole weight, which wasn't much these days, he mused, as he tried to force the pole into the hardened ground. It stayed upright and the fence was a barrier once more, albeit a lank and twisted one.

He looked out across the empty green field. It had once been part of his family's land, but years of financial hardship and his inability to manage the bills meant he had been given no choice but to sell up. The last of his elderly horses had recently been euthanised and the land was surplus to requirements. When Meadowbridge Homes had approached him with an offer to purchase the land, he'd eagerly accepted. He wasn't keen on his beautiful farm becoming shadowed by a characterless housing estate, but the pay-out he received meant he would be able to stay in the family home and at least maintain some dignity.

His decision wasn't so well received by the rest of the villagers though and angry protests ensued, with Tom being labelled the Antichrist who'd allowed it all to happen. However, that was six years ago now and with every planning notice declined the lush green field had remained unspoilt. His relationship with the locals, though fractious at times, was much better and his daily trip to the village to deliver eggs was welcomed once again.

He looked down at the now empty wicker basket. If stacked carefully, it held exactly 60 eggs and not a single egg more. It had been his wife's basket and he recalled how she would scuttle outside at the break of dawn in her fluffy slippers to let out the hens whilst she gathered the eggs. It would sometimes take her three trips to decant the eggs into a larger basket inside the farmhouse. Tom would then carefully load the basket into his truck and deliver them around town: the village store, May's café, the junior school, Mrs Crompton at her B&B, the fire station and the butcher's shop were all regular customers. He would sometimes have enough to service the neighbouring village too. Brown's eggs were a popular commodity and the family's main source of income.

Though well into his seventies, Tom didn't want to retire. He enjoyed working and the meagre sum he earned from selling his eggs was the difference between five months in a freezing cold farmhouse or a good supply of coal for his fire. The money he'd received from the developers was long gone. At first, he'd enjoyed having money in the bank; he had replaced the roof on the barn and invested in a new, much bigger coop for the hens, as well as a better van in which to make his deliveries. He indulged in the odd takeaway meal once a week, whilst his patronage at The Red Lion was a lot more frequent. But, of course, those six years had nibbled away at his windfall and now there was nothing left. The eggs were his only income and chronic arthritis in his knees meant the van was left to rust away in the yard.

He plodded up the overgrown path to the house, casting a disapproving look at the cluster of hens as he passed them.

Pushing open the heavy wooden door, he stepped into the kitchen and placed the basket down on the large oak table. He reached into his pocket, pulled out a handful of coins and looked at them. 'Seven pounds,' he said out loud. Shaking his head, he spread the coins out on the table. 'Seven pounds,' he repeated.

Tom owned around a hundred chickens, most of which were getting older and way past production. He never slaughtered his old girls though, preferring to keep them as pets; they were good company and relatively cheap to feed. He'd recently invested in some new hens and the seller had boasted that they were from a long line of great layers. Scepticism soon crept in when he'd open the coop each morning and the haul was sparse. Nevertheless, he fed them well and some days were better than others.

Sighing, he scuffed over towards a steel kettle sitting on an old stove in the corner. Filling it with water, he placed it back onto the hob and lit the gas.

He stepped over to the fridge and pulled out a bottle of milk. Lifting the lid, he cautiously sniffed it. Then, satisfied it hadn't gone sour, he poured a generous splash into a mug.

Other than the milk and a small chunk of cheese, the fridge was empty. He withdrew the cheese and opened the bread bin beside the fridge. Inside was a small loaf of uncut bread and a rustic roll. He reached for the roll and pulled the sliding hatch down on the bread bin. With his bare hands, he pulled the roll apart and inserted the chunk of cheese. As he did so a whistling sound emitted from the kettle and he removed it from the hob. Placing a strainer over his cup, he lumped a dollop of tea into it and proceeded to pour the steaming water.

Slumping back down in the rickety chair, he took a big bite out of his roll. As he sat with his tea in hand, he glanced through the window. The beautiful, blue sky was quickly disappearing behind a bank of ominous-looking black clouds.

The busted fence will have to wait, he thought to himself, and moved over to a more comfortable armchair where he promptly fell asleep.

Woken suddenly by a crack of thunder, Tom sat bolt upright. The rain was hammering down. Looking up at the clock on the wall – it read 4:40 – he slowly stood up, placing his palm on the small of his back as pain seared up his spine. He reached for his tattered old raincoat hanging on the stand inside the door and made his way outside.

He scanned the farmyard for his chickens, but there were none to be seen. He tutted and carried on over to the yard, but there wasn't a single hen in sight.

Tom started to panic. He crossed the yard, then his eyes fell upon the half-open door to the barn. He slowly hobbled over and a wave of relief swept over him as he saw the clutch of hens all safely huddled together on the floor inside.

The rain was lashing down outside and he decided to let them stay in the barn rather than try to herd them all back to their coop.

He stepped over towards a stack of bound hay bales and with great effort pulled one down. Reaching for a knife that was hanging behind him on the barn wall, he cut the string with one swift motion. Then he returned the knife to its hook and, plunging his hands into the bale, he pulled apart large sections and proceeded to spread the loose hay across the floor.

'That'll do for tonight, girls,' he called out cheerfully. Pulling up the collar on his coat, he closed up the barn and quickly made his way across the yard and back into the house.

Pausing in the doorway, Tom removed his coat and shook it to get as much of the rain off as possible. Then he closed the door and hung it up on the stand.

Making himself another cup of tea, he sat down. There was a wad of envelopes wedged in the toast rack in the centre of the table. Tom reached over and took them out, flicking through and dropping each one nonchalantly.

He stopped and examined the last envelope in his hand. Curling his lip, he hesitated before ripping it open. It was a letter from the hospital's oncology department. He studied the words, but he wasn't really absorbing them.

Mavis at the post office had insisted he go for a check-up after noticing he had lost a great deal of weight. He'd agreed, but just to be sure he actually attended it she took him there in her car.

The wait for the results of his blood test had finally been over, but he'd left the letter on the table for weeks amongst the bills and junk mail.

Tom sighed and screwed the letter into a ball. He looked over to the fireplace and lined up his shot. As he was about to toss the paper ball across the room an ear splitting crack of thunder startled him and he dropped it to the floor.

He shuddered as a sudden down draft blew in through the cracks in the window frame.

Standing up, he looked out of the window towards the barn. Satisfied his chickens would be safe in there for the night, he picked up his mug and made his way to the bedroom. Still fully clothed, he carefully climbed into bed and sat propped up against the headboard. He flicked on the bedside lamp and reached for a paperback book left open upside down on the cabinet and started to read.

The thunder was unrelenting and Tom cocked his ear to hear the rhythmic plink-plink sound of raindrops coming in through the ceiling and dripping into the saucepan he used for such occasions. He sighed. *Another* job to have to deal with.

He read for an hour, by which time the thunder had become a distant rumble and the rain had eased to a stop. He put the book back onto the bedside cabinet and shuffled down under the blankets. It didn't take long before he was sound asleep.

As the sun rose, Tom Brown's farm was dappled with the sunlight glistening through the ancient oak trees bordering his land. The resident cockerel poked his head out of the coop, strutted down the slope and, stretching out his neck, let out a raucous cock-a-doodle-do.

Tom's eyes flickered open and he squinted at the shard of light beaming in through the gap in his tattered old brown curtains. The sudden urge to relieve his bladder foisted itself upon him and he threw the blankets aside.

As he turned over in bed he groaned with pain; he had cramp in his leg and his lower back was burning. He slowly hoisted himself up and rubbed vigorously at his leg until the pins and needles sensation subsided. With a loud sigh, he stood up and hobbled to the bathroom. He just reached the toilet in time and a wave of relief swept over him as he dribbled into the lavatory.

Looking at his weathered face in the mirror, Tom stroked his chin and ran the back of his hand across his cheek. He reached for an old bristled brush and ran it under the tap. Dabbing it into his shaving soap, leaving bristles embedded in the cake, he started to cover his cheeks in soapy foam. He searched the top of the sink for his blade, but it wasn't there. He stood for a moment with a puzzled expression on his face.

'Where's my old razor?' he muttered to himself. As he moved around the bathroom scanning every surface, soap dripped from his face onto the stone tiled floor. His eyes caught sight of the shiny, hinged blade on the windowsill and as he stepped forward to retrieve it he slipped in the soapy puddle on the floor. Shocked and disoriented, Tom grabbed hold of the towel rail on the wall, just managing to keep himself upright. He sat down on the side of the bath, his heart racing. 'Phew! That was close!' he said out loud.

He pondered for a moment. What would have happened if he *did* fall? How long before someone found him? How long before he was missed? It was a sobering thought that sent chills throughout his body. Tom was a proud man and the thought of being found weeks or months after death in goodness knows what state horrified him. 'I must be more careful,' he told himself. He stood up and took the razor from the windowsill.

With deliberate care and meticulous accuracy, Tom shaved his face before making his way downstairs to the kitchen.

He filled the kettle and lit the hob. Flipping open the breadbin he pulled out the small loaf. Selecting a serrated knife from the drawer, he cut the end slice and placed it on the table. Then he shuffled over the fridge and removed the bottle of milk. Frowning at the empty void, he felt disappointed at the lack of filling or even some butter for his bread.

Suddenly the cockerel crowed out in the yard and Tom chuckled. 'Of course! Silly me!' He stepped into his shoes and made his way out into the yard.

The cockerel crowed again as Tom approached the coop. 'Alright old fella, I'm coming.' Tom flicked open the latch on the coop and the cockerel ran out and across the yard. He fluttered up onto an upturned wooden crate and bellowed out his loudest cock-a-doodle-do.

Tom walked over to the barn and opened the door. The hens were all sat in a huddle, seemingly unaware that morning had come.

'Good morning, ladies,' Tom announced. The hens started to rouse and one by one they got up and ran out into the yard. Tom rustled about in the hay he'd laid out the night before. He frowned. Moving along he felt beneath the hay as he crossed the floor. His eyes lit up as he reached the middle of the pile and his fingers felt the freshly laid egg. 'Bingo!' he exclaimed.

Picking up the precious offering he made his way back to the farmhouse where the kettle was whistling away frantically. He lifted it off the hob and placed a frying pan over the flame. Cracking the egg into the pan he smiled as he watched it bubble and turn white. He made his tea and scooped the fried egg from the pan, laid it out gently on the slice of bread and folded it in half. Then he sat down and contentedly tucked into his egg sandwich.

His eyes fell upon the wicker basket in the middle of the table and he looked up at the clock on the wall, which was now showing 05:30. He wiped his mouth with the back of his hand and picked up the basket.

Trudging back out to the coop, Tom felt a little despondent. He hoped a second visit to the barn would be more bountiful if he dug deeper into the makeshift roost.

He stepped inside and resumed his daily routine of gathering eggs. As he worked his way round, he carefully placed the eggs into the basket. He reached the end of the hay spread out on the floor and the harvest barely covered the bottom of the basket. Bemused, Tom doubled back and checked the floor again, but there was nothing. Determined he would not be consumed by sadness and disappointment, Tom smiled. 'At least the firemen will get their breakfast.' He chuckled to himself.

Tom closed the barn door and, with his basket carrying less than two-dozen eggs, he made his way down to the village.

Tom reached the fire station to find that the shutters on the old slabbed building were up and the single engine that served Blechnum and the neighbouring village of Egsa-Aston was gone.

He stepped into the open bay and called out. 'Hello? Anybody home?' There was no reply. He looked around and noticed a small cardboard box on a table in the corner. He took out the eggs one at a time and carefully placed them in the box. He called out again, but accepting there was nobody there he left.

71

As he walked across the road he could see May waving to him from the doorway of her café. He ambled over to her and as he got closer he lifted the basket and turned it on its side to reveal its emptiness. 'I'm sorry, May, my girls didn't do so well this morning.'

May smiled warmly. 'That's okay, Tom. Maybe tomorrow, eh?'

Tom returned the smile. 'You're top of my list.'

'Just wait there a minute,' May said as she slipped behind the door. She returned with a white paper bag and handed it to Tom. He opened it and beamed a toothless smile.

'Bread pudding! My favourite. Thank you, May.'

She planted a soft kiss on his cheek and turned to go back into the cafe. 'See you tomorrow, love,' she said as the door closed.

Tom reached the gate fronting his farm and let out a loud exasperated sigh. The boundary fence was down again and his chickens were strewn across the open fields. Some were disappearing into the woodland beyond and in the distance he could see a lone fox skulking about in the long grass and heading towards his precious hens.

He quickly stepped over the fence and his foot got caught in the wire. He stumbled forward and landed flat on his front with a dull thud.

For a moment Tom thought this was it; this is where he would lay until the Grim Reaper came and took him.

He closed his eyes and relaxed his body on the cold damp earth. It was only a matter of seconds, but Tom felt an ethereal glow that seemed to whisk him away for much longer. He thought of Rosie, his wife. He hoped she'd be there waiting for him.

Suddenly he was wrenched back to reality and the searing pain in his knees, coupled with the burning sensation in his ankle, hit him like a ton of bricks. He exhaled deeply and opened his eyes to see the chickens scattered and running in blind panic as the fox nimbly chased them. He placed his palms to the soggy ground and with all his strength pushed himself up onto his knees. Ignoring the pain, he stood quickly and with a force fuelled by adrenaline he clambered over the clods of earth towards the chaotic scene.

The fox was leaping and darting backwards and forwards. The chickens were fluttering and running in all directions, soft underbelly feathers wafting into the air like the remnants of a pillow fight.

Tom shouted 'Shoo! Get out of here!'

The fox stopped and turned to face him. Then, with a flick of its bushy tail, it sprinted off up the bank and over the hill out of sight.

Tom looked about frantically. The feathers slowly fluttered to the ground as the cacophony of frightened squawking dimmed to agitated caws.

It looked as though most of his flock were present. He spoke softly in an effort to calm them and scanned the area in a vain attempt to collate the hens that were now dispersing again and headed in the direction of the farm.

Out of the corner of his eye he could see the rooster pecking about in the shrubbery where the woodland met the field. He turned to watch the hens running back towards the farm and beckoned the cockerel to follow. 'Come on you, let's get back to the farm,' he said breathlessly. The cockerel paid no attention and carried on foraging and scraping the ground with his clawed feet.

Tom reached into his pocket and retrieved the now flattened slab of bread pudding. He broke off a corner and tossed it towards the cockerel. Tom started to walk towards him, trying to coax him with the tasty offering. This had the opposite effect and the large, golden bird sprinted off into the woods.

'Oh, for Christ's sake!' Tom exclaimed.

He followed the rooster into the trees, pushing aside large ferns to make a path. He got deeper into the forest, but the rooster was nowhere to be seen. He was about to give up and turn around when he saw a clearing with a beautiful stone-built well. The sun was shining down on the well, casting a spotlight across the tiled roof.

Tom had lived in Blechnum his whole life and had played in the woods as a child. He had heard about the well, but for some reason, up until this moment he had never actually set eyes on it.

He approached slowly, his ankle throbbing with every footstep. He stopped at the stone surround and placed his palms down on the rim. He looked into the well. It was black, there was no bottom that Tom could see and it seemed to go on forever. He looked up at the handle; a short, frayed section of rope dangled where there once would have been a bucket. Crudely nailed to the peaked wooden roof was a carved sign bearing the words **MAKE A WISH**.

Tom chuckled and looked around him. There was a silence and serenity he had never experienced before and all the thoughts and worries for his fugitive rooster had completely dissipated.

He fumbled in his trouser pockets for a coin and pulled out a handful of lint and some bread pudding crumbs. 'Oh, dash it!' he said. 'Can I owe you a shilling?' he added jovially, addressing the well.

He laughed heartily and took a deep breath. 'I wish my hens would lay loads more eggs,' he called into the vast chasm.

His words echoed back up at him, trailing off to a faint "eggs... eggs... eggs...".

Tom sighed and then suddenly felt a wave of embarrassment. Nobody had seen him or heard him, but he couldn't shake the uncomfortable feeling that he was somehow under scrutiny. He took one last look at the well and made his way back through the trees to his farm.

When he reached the yard he scowled as he saw the cockerel proudly perched up high on the roof of the coop. He waved his fist at him and crossed to the barn. The hens were inside and he opened the door wide.

'Come on you lot. Out!'

He waved his arms and herded the chickens out through the door and back to their coop. The hens obediently scuttled inside, hopping through the opening to the mesh enclosure one at a time. Once they were all safely inside, Tom closed the door, but in his flustered state he forgot to slide the locking latch.

He felt absolutely exhausted and it took all his strength to haul himself into the farmhouse. He pushed open the door and lumbered inside. It wasn't even midday, but Tom was hurting and unfeasibly tired, so he carried on through the kitchen and clambered up the stairs to bed.

During the night, as the clouds moved to reveal a full moon, there was unusual activity outside in the hen house. The noise coming from the coop was enough to wake the dead, but Tom didn't stir.

The hens were agitated and sat in orderly lines on the shelves of the roost, but the sound inside was deafening.

They started to shuffle about as they involuntarily began to lay eggs by the dozen.

The shelves were filling up and bowing under the weight, and as the eggs started to overflow, the hens were forced to jump down into the open space of the pen. As they frantically walked around in circles around the perimeter of the enclosure, eggs continued to drop. The pen soon started to fill and the hens were being squashed atop the pile as it stacked up to the roof of the enclosure. Yolk was oozing through the wire mess as the eggs got crushed.

All of a sudden, the door to the coop was flung open and eggs cascaded out into the yard. They glistened in the moonlight like a vast cobbled seafront.

The hens became more and more distressed and were scuttling aimlessly around the yard. They ran towards the farmhouse and, seizing the opportunity to seek sanctuary inside, they scuttled in through the door Tom had carelessly left open that afternoon.

They ran into the kitchen, pushing past each other like eager shoppers during the January sale. They flocked inside, running across the floor and underneath the table, dropping eggs everywhere they went. A few of them hopped up onto Tom's old chair, the eggs rolling off the tattered seat and smashing on the floor. As the stone tiles of the kitchen floor disappeared under a carpet of eggs, a group of the hens rushed up the stairs, and the noise as hundreds of eggs tumbled down the stairs behind them like an ovum landslide was deafening.

One of the hens tried to return downstairs, but the entire lower half of the house was filled to the seams with eggs. She clucked with fear and hurried along the hallway, following several others into the bedroom. The landing was filled with eggs and as the birds ran manically around the bedroom the doorway became blocked.

They flapped their wings and fluttered up onto the bed as the eggs continued to fall, rolling off the bed and onto the floor, filling the tiny room.

Tom woke suddenly as he felt the sharp claw of a hen scratched his face. Startled he sat up and his eyes widened at the sight before him. Then he felt a crushing pain in his chest as the bed became buried under a mountain of eggs. He looked up at the ceiling and took one last breath as his eyes focussed on the blurred glowing outline of his beloved Rosie smiling down at him.

THE CRUISE THAT NEVER ENDED

Sandra Ower

(Introduction by Rebecca Xibalba)

Dave stood by the printer in his office, catching the sheets of paper as they fell. He gathered them up into a neat pile and slipped them into a plastic folder.

There was far too much going on in the building today. A new air conditioning system was being fitted and the noise was becoming intolerable. Dave had decided he would make The Sly Fox his office today; not only was it considerably quieter, they also made a sensational lamb hotpot, and their draft beer was the perfect accompaniment.

He left the building and made his way along Mafeking Parade towards the pub. As he stepped inside, the barman acknowledged his arrival. 'Afternoon, Dave. You're early today.'

'Aye, working lunch,' he replied. 'Have you still got that beer on tap? The honey one?'

'Bumble Brew?' the barman enquired.

'Yeah, that's the one'

The barman moved along the bar and reached for a pint glass. He poured the drink and placed it on the bar. 'Three quid mate,' he declared.

Dave pulled a handful of change from his pocket and selected three one-pound coins. He handed them to the barman and took the drink. 'Cheers, pal.'

The barman nodded and Dave took a seat in a booth at the far corner of the pub. He took a big sip from his beer, which left a giant moustache adorning his top lip. He let out a loud 'ahhhh' of satisfaction and licked his lips, then he put down the glass and pushed it to the far end of the table. Placing the folder in front of him, he withdrew the paperwork. He felt in his inside pocket and pulled out a pair of spectacles.

Reading through the multitude of pages, Dave paused. He whipped out two pages and put them to one side before carrying on. He took another big gulp of his beer and wiped his mouth with the back of his hand. Reaching the last page, he placed the wad back inside the folder and retrieved the two pages he had separated earlier. The pages contained technical drawings; plans for a development. He placed them down and studied them intently. He reached into his pocket again and pulled out a ballpoint pen. He circled an area on the plans and tapped his lip with the butt of the pen. Frowning, he sat back in the chair and scanned the ceiling, almost as if he was looking up there for an answer to a question.

The moment was abruptly disturbed as a voice said, 'Penny for 'em!'

Dave looked down and straight into the cleavage of a young woman in a tight fitting top and short skirt. 'Candice! What are you doing skulking around here?'

The woman sat down beside him. 'Looking for something hot and tasty,' she replied with a wink.

Dave looked around and leaned in to kiss her on the lips.

'Are they the Meadowbridge plans?' Candice asked, pointing to the drawings.

'Yeah,' Dave replied with a heavy sigh.

'Problems?' Candice asked.

'Yeah, kinda.' Dave indicated the area on the plans that he had circled. 'There's a water source here that wasn't mentioned in the previous survey. I'm going to have to check it out before we can sign this off, just in case it's drainage or some kind of underground spring. We can't go building over a geyser!'

Candice frowned. 'Geyser?'

'It's like… oh, never mind. Whatever it is, I'll have to check it out before we let the diggers in. He placed the plans back into his folder and downed the rest of his beer.

'Are you going?' Candice asked.

'Yeah I'd better crack on,' Dave replied.

'Maybe see you tonight?'

Dave smiled. 'I'll text you later.' He bent down and kissed Candice passionately before strolling out of the pub.

Half an hour later, having parked up in a dusty lay-by, and deftly avoiding the muddy puddles from last night's deluge, he opened the rickety old gate affronting Blechnum Meadow.

He walked across the field and pulled out the plans from the folder. He looked from left to right and after consulting the drawings he headed off to the right where a line of bushes bordered the woodland. Finding a gap in the hedgerow he entered the woods.

It was still very soft underfoot and he tutted at his muddied shoes. After a short walk through the trees he spotted a small area to the right, which stood out amongst the deep foliage. Tucked behind dense bushes was a copse which, despite the makeshift wall of tall trees guarding it, was brightly illuminated by the sun. He stepped through and smiled. 'There you are!' he exclaimed loudly as the stone well came into view.

He pulled out his pen and jotted some notes down on the plans. Then he pulled out his phone and took a few photos.

Stepping up to the well, he looked down into the darkness. He turned the handle on the side and the crank turned. He examined it closely; the rope and bucket had long since gone.

Dave turned and made his way back to his car. Before he got in, he pulled out a handkerchief and wiped his shoes. Holding the filthy piece of cloth aloft, he thoughtlessly tossed it onto the ground. Then, starting the engine, he closed the door and drove off.

Pulling into a service station a couple of miles up the road, Dave stopped at the drive-through and ordered a coffee. He parked up in a bay and opened his mobile. Sighing, he looked through the photos of the well and sipped at the coffee.

He closed the photo app and opened up Google. Typing "Blechnum Well" into the search field, he scrolled through until his eyes fell upon the words **"Haunted well" responsible for missing school children!**. Clicking the link, he read through the article with interest. It turned out that it was a newspaper story dating back to 1971 that had been uploaded to a paranormal website. Dave slowly sipped at his coffee as he continued reading. There were several police reports from the 1970s claiming that the children who had been on a cruise – part-educational, part-holiday – had disappeared, and their ship, the SS Catherine, was later located sunk. Everyone who had been aboard was presumed dead. Dave scrolled through photographs of the school class and several pictures of the dredged-up wreck of the Catherine. He stared in semi-disbelief at a reprint of a journal purportedly written by one of the girls on the trip. The caption stated that it had washed up on a beach in France in 1976 and, being sealed in a bottle, it had been perfectly intact.

Dave started to read…

MY CRUISE
MAY 1971

May 3rd 1971

The ship was late arriving in port today and all the girls were getting impatient. I have been looking forward to this cruise. Finally we sighted SS Catherine coming into port. The loud voice of Miss Hartweed sounded out, so all the girls hurried to board the ship. We were shown to our dormitaries in which the beds were spaced out in rows. They look comfortable. Beside each bed there is a cupboard. After unpacking my case I went up on deck. The sky looks stormy tonight.

♥

May 4th 1971

Last night a storm blew up and I could not sleep. But this morning I was awakened by the screeches of the seagulls and Miss Hartweed coming in, shouting that breakfast was ready. This afternoon we arrived in Malta. I scouted around the shops and bought a few things, then came back to the ship. We left Malta earlier this evening. The sea was calm. I decided to explore the ship. I walked along a corridor and I heard laughter coming from the room at the end. Looking through the keyhole, I saw three men smoking cigars and playing cards. One of them had money piled up in front of him and it looked like he was winning. Then a hand touched my shoulder. I looked up to find it was Miss Hartweed. She led me to the dormitory. I'm now going to bed.

♥

May 5th 1971

Last night a scream from the cabin next door awoke me. There was a smell of smoke. Miss Hartweed rushed out to see what had happened. The place was full of smoke. A young girl of about 18 lay of the floor. The curtains were on fire and there was the stench of cigars and beer. The Captain rushed in. The fire had spread along the corridor. The Captain sounded the alarm to abandon ship. Miss Hartweed counted us. We were then led to the lifeboats. I jumped in. As we

floated away, the ship exploded,
sending up flames and smoke
and it sank. Our lovely cruise is
over.

♥

May 7th 1971

For two days we have floated,
without food. Four of the girls
have been ill. On the second night
a mist moved towards us. The
other boats could not be seen. All
was quiet except for the movement
of the oars. The Captain kept
watch while the girls slept. The
sound of a motor woke us and
through the mist I could see a
ship. The Captain shouted, but the
people on board could not hear us.
They were heading straight
towards us! Then the boat
carrying Miss Hartweed appeared.
The Captain tried to warn them
that a ship was approaching, but
they did not hear. The lifeboat was

heading into the path of the ship!
The girls shouted and shouted,
but it did no good. It was too late –
the ship crashed into Miss
Hartweed's boat. When the ship
had passed, we looked for
survivors, but there were none. The
remains of the lifeboat sank. The
Captain led us in a prayer, then
we continued on. I am hoping that
by morning the mist will have
cleared and we will find land.

♥

<u>May 8th 1971</u>

Early this morning a shout from
the Captain awoke us. We had
reached an island! The sun was
shining and the island was
covered with palm trees and sand.
After leaving the lifeboats,
everyone explored the island. Then
we started to collect leaves and
branches to build a hut with. We

are now inside and settling down for the night.

♥

May 9th 1971

Last night I dreamt of all the things I would do this morning and of how long we would be on the island. I woke early to find the Captain was already up. He had been fishing, but hadn't had much success. The girls went looking for food, and found coconuts and berries. One girl found a pure water stream.

♥

May 15th 1971

Several days have gone by. Not one ship or boat has been seen. We have been on the island a week now and there had been no sign of life. After having a dinner of crushed berries, we went for a walk around the island. It is huge and there is still much we have not explored. We had not seen any animals yet, but as we went further into the trees, a flock of tiny birds flew by us. Something had frightened them. The Captain halted. "What's the matter?" someone asked. "Drums," he replied. Then one of the girls screamed. There in the tree above them was a puma. The Captain told us to move back slowly. The youngest girl, Jill, ran screaming. The puma jumped and attacked her! Then, to everyone's surprise, four natives with spears appeared and killed the puma. Jill was not hurt, only scratched. The natives seemed friendly. We were taken to their village where we were welcomed by their King, whose name was Kuga. Two native girls gave us two baskets of fruit. We said thank you. We

were then taken back to our camp
on the beach.

♥

May 18th 1971

Many natives have come to visit
us each day. Some even built huts
on the beach. This morning one of
the women ran up to me shouting
and crying. She pulled at my
sleeve as if she wanted me to come
with her. I followed her to a hut. I
went in and there on the bed was a
boy aged about nine. He was
covered in a black rash. His
mother threw herself in front of
me clearly needing help. What
could I do? The black fever had
struck! The boy died this evening.

♥

May 20th 1971

Two more days have gone by.
Many of the natives have died of

the fever. This afternoon the
Captain suddenly collapsed. I ran
to see what had happened. He had
the fever! Two of the girls carried
him to the hut. There is no cure for
this terrible fever!

❤

May 21st 1971

Last night, I slept in the open,
praying that the Captain would
get better. This morning I awoke
early. The first thing I did was go
into the hut. The Captain did not
move. I felt his pulse. He was dead.
I fear we will never escape this
island now.

❤

Spring 1974

We are no longer sure exactly
what the date is. For three years

we have lived on this island. No ships have passed. Today Jill shouted out that there was a raft or something floating on the shore. She rushed down to the beach to see what it was. It was a kind of box. Jill opened it. There, lying on a bundle of rags, was a puppy, half-starved and as cold as ice. "Give the puppy to me," I said. Its fur was cold and stiff. Two natives fetched a bowl of water and some meat. We watched the puppy eat it. In two seconds the meat was gone. The puppy then ran away into the trees. I ran after him. Eventually I found him asleep in some long grass. I picked him up and carried him back to the hut. We have decided to call him Rusty.

♥

This afternoon Jill and I took Rusty for a walk. We went further afield than we have done before. There we sighted some caves. Rusty ran ahead. The caves were huge and dark. Then a bark from the cave ahead brought us rushing in. Rusty had dug a hole for some reason. I looked to see what he was doing. He had dug up a box! Jill found a stone and broke the lock. Inside the box was a heap of stones and a map. It was a treasure map, written in Latin. Luckily I know how to read Latin. It showed the way from the cave, through a tunnel to an underground chamber and indicated there was treasure buried there. We took the map and decided to look for this so-called treasure. We followed the instructions and found the tunnel and the room – and, luckily, a spade! We took turns in digging. Even Rusty helped. Then we dug up a box. It was heavy. We dragged it through the tunnel, out into the light. We opened it with a stone. Inside was a sack. I emptied the sack onto the

sand. To our surprise, out fell
rubies, diamond necklaces, gold
rings, bracelets, five gold cups
and all other kinds of riches. I put
everything back into the sack,
then we returned to our hut on the
beach. The natives welcomed us
back. I took the sack into the hut
and put it under the bed. Then we
sat down for tea. While we were
eating, one of the natives ran by.
He was wearing some of the
treasure. Two of the girls ran after
him. They managed to catch him.
Then they put the jewels back into
the sack.

❤

Summer 1974

This morning I was awakened by
a native. He said he had seen a
boat on the sea on the other side of
the island. I went to look. Two
men were leaving the boat in a
rubber dinghy. I told the natives

to keep hidden. The two men went into the cave where we had found the treasure. I thought of a plan to scare them away, so I called all the natives together. I told them to dress up and use the berry juice to make war-paint. Then the natives went into the cave. I heard a scream and the two men rushed out, followed by the natives. The men forgot their dinghy, and swam out to their boat and sailed away. We now have a boat!

❤

Today is the day we are going to leave this beautiful island that we have lived on for three years. This afternoon the natives danced and we said farewell. The natives gave us presents and food. I then collected the treasure and we set off in the dinghy. The natives waved us goodbye. I am so glad to be leaving, but it was also sad to

say goodbye to the natives who
have become our friends.

♥

August 4th 1974

We floated about for two days
before a ship was sighted and we
were picked up. We were saved!
The ship is SS Princess. The
Captain's name is Laurence
Smith. We told him the whole
story. We were then shown to our
cabins and given new clothes.

♥

August 11th 1974

We have been aboard now for
seven days and we haven't seen
anything but more and more
water. We only know how many

days have passed by counting the nights.

♥

<u>August 15th 1974</u>

A few more days have passed and people are starting to panic. The kitchen has stopped making dinners – we are only given one meal a day and most of the time it's tinned food like spaghetti, baked beans, Pease Pudding and plum tomatoes. The staff have told us that we must be careful how much water we drink as that is also now running low. It isn't much fun really and all I can think is, why did I go to that stupid well and why did I wish for this cruise to last forever? My parents may have been a drag, but I would much rather be home with them and my annoying sister right now. This cruise is really boring and I am so fed up with spaghetti!

♥

<u>August 19th 1974</u>

Another 4 days have passed and
today the Captain of the Princess
came and told us that there was
something wrong with the ship.
He said the compass is broken
and it looks like we are going
round in circles. I don't really
understand it, but it certainly
feels like there is no land in sight
and, when I look out at the sea,
everything just looks the same.

♥

<u>August 21st 1974</u>

Some of the girls from my class
are missing. I don't know where
they are. There seem to be a lot less
people on the ship. Maybe they're
staying in their cabins until we
reach land. I'm starting to feel
really tired now. The meals have
got even smaller and we have to

take our cups to the kitchen in the morning for water and we can't have any more so we have to make it last. I managed to go up on deck today. It was a really hot day and I couldn't stay there long. Everything still looks the same outside.

♥

August 23rd 1974

Another day has passed and I have decided to send my journal out to sea. I don't think we will ever make it back to England now and I hope it will reach home so my parents know what happened to me. I have found an old bottle in the kitchen, there was no one there to stop me taking it, I don't know where they've gone. If you find this please contact my parents. They live in Essex. My door number is 80, it's Southend Road, the house with the roses outside.

Dave closed the web page and stared out of the car window.

He was suddenly engulfed by an inexplicable wave of sadness, and he no longer felt quite so enthusiastic about the Meadowbridge project.

He started the car, pulled slowly out of the drive-through and set off back to the office.

THE UNDERSTUDY

Rebecca Xibalba

The inner lenses of his compact binoculars fogged and Alex sighed with exasperation. 'Not *now*!' he exclaimed.

He had been sat on this tree stump for almost an hour, his backside was numb, his neck ached and just as a glimpse of the prize he had come here for was presented before him, the damned binoculars fogged and robbed him of the moment.

A pair of pigeons were cooing as they bobbed their heads in courtship a few feet from him. He looked at them and frowned; were they mocking him, he wondered? Laughing at his misfortune?

He could have got nearer, he would have had a much clearer view if he'd been down there. He might even have had the chance to take a few photographs. But the open air theatre in Hyde Park always attracted a crowd and Alex never felt comfortable in a crowd.

Opera wasn't what he would call entertainment either. He didn't understand the language, he hated the pomp and ceremony of it and, most of all, his father loved it, so that alone was enough to make him despise it inordinately.

But this opera was different. Yes, it was Italian and the overacting of the male lead was as masculine as a lace handkerchief. However this production had one very special feature: an aria by the one and only Miranda D'Angelo, three minutes and thirty seconds long, billed as a cameo appearance. The amateur production had cleverly cast West End star D'Angelo to undertake the role of Sophia, the tragic wife of

104

Antonio, who is shot on stage during her performance. This piece of casting had guaranteed a sell out and there wasn't an empty seat in the outside auditorium. That's why Alex was watching his heroine through binoculars, from a hilltop 200 feet away.

He frantically wiped at the lenses with the edge of his jumper as the distant sound of Miranda's voice drifted up to him on the breeze. He raised the binoculars to his face again and smiled as he focused them on the centre of the stage. Miranda was just approaching the crescendo and Alex held his breath as he watched her intently. His heart beat heavy in his chest and he exhaled slowly through his nose.

Miranda hit the high note and a shot rang out through the air, disturbing the pigeons, who took flight and startled Alex. He dropped the binoculars. 'Damn!' he hissed. He scrabbled around in the long grass, but by the time he'd found them he could hear the rapturous applause and looked up to see the red velvet curtains had been drawn around the circular stage.

'Get out of my way!'

With her white dress flapping behind her in the breeze, Miranda pushed her way through the cast and crew who were gathered in the back stage area inside a large marquee.

A stout man stepped out in front of Miranda and she came to an abrupt halt. 'What the hell are...' She faltered. 'Oh, Sir Anthony, I'm sorry. Did you enjoy the show?' she asked, extending her cheek as he leant towards her for a kiss.

'Absolutely astounding, Ms D'Angelo. It nigh on brought me to tears!'

Miranda flashed him a smile. 'Oh, I'm delighted to hear that. I hope I'll see you at the show in London in September. It's one of Gervais Macron's tragedies and I'm playing the lead.'

'You most certainly will, my dear...' Anthony trailed off as his attention was drawn to a group of people on the other side of the marquee. 'Sylvia, darling!' he called out as he casually walked away from Miranda.

'Charming!' Miranda uttered under her breath. Gathering up the bottom of her dress into her hands, she marched off towards a fifth wheel trailer that was parked up behind the stage.

As she reached the makeshift dressing room, she adjusted the crooked laminated cardboard star that had been crudely adhered to the outside with Blu Tack. She tutted and pushed open the door.

Inside the trailer was a circular seating area with a sheepskin rug and a small table in the middle. The table was laid out with a resplendent fruit platter. Miranda pulled off a grape and popped it into her mouth. As she bit into the skin she screwed up her eyes and recoiled at the bitter taste. Spitting it out onto the rug, she stomped off into the bedroom, slamming the door shut behind her.

Alex had made his way down the hill and managed to locate the backstage area, which was enclosed in a ring of steel fencing covered by blue tarpaulin. He could hear voices and laughter from behind the plastic coated barrier and listened carefully as he tried to decipher what they were saying. A woman was talking loudly and several men could be heard laughing every time she stopped. The brash northern dialect of this woman assured Alex it was not Miranda; his idol had a softly spoken voice with a slight raspy sound and she was definitely not from the north.

He edged round the outside of the fence looking for a break in the cover so that he might at least get a little peek at the gathering inside. As he walked slowly around the barrier he failed to notice another fan stood by the fence, holding an autograph book and biro, eagerly waiting. Alex bumped straight into him and the man dropped his book and pen.

'Oh, I'm sorry!' Alex exclaimed.

The man bent down to retrieve his items. As he stood up, he repositioned his spectacles and glared at Alex. 'You should look where you're going,' he sneered.

'Yeah, sorry mate,' Alex replied.

'And where exactly *were* you going?' the man asked with an accusatory tone.

'Oh I was just hoping to get a quick glance of the cast, maybe a little photo of...'

The other man interrupted. 'Miranda?' He grinned at Alex, showing a mouthful of decaying teeth. 'You'll never get a photo of Miranda. She's a superstar, you know. I've been a fan of hers for 20 years. She knows me and always smiles when she sees me. But she never stops for photos.'

Alex nodded politely. 'Right.' He started to step away from the man, but as he moved towards the corner and attempted to slip around and out of sight, the man followed him.

'I first saw Miranda in a local pantomime. She was Cinderella. That was 20 years ago.'

Alex quickened his pace.

'Then I saw her in "The Lion King",' the annoying man continued. She played a gazelle. Then I went to Manchester to see her in…'

There was a metallic scraping sound and both men stopped. They turned and hurried back just as a car door slammed shut and the Range Rover started to reverse away from them.

A burly security guard was stood between the gap in the fencing and eyed the two men. 'Can I help you gentlemen?' he asked in a gruff voice.

Alex spoke. 'Was that Miranda D'Angelo?'

The guard smiled and without a word pulled the fence closed and locked it.

Alex snapped his head back angrily and stared at the bespectacled geek, who was tucking the small hardback autograph book back into his satchel. He looked up and shrugged. 'Oh well,' he said nonchalantly and strolled off towards the road.

Alex sighed. He looked back at the fence and then turned to see the other man disappearing off out of sight. Resigned to the fact he wasn't going to see the beautiful Miranda, he took off up the road towards the underground station.

Tracey Tranter stood in front of a long, free-standing mirror in her studio flat in Camden Town.

She turned to the left, then to the right, then back to the left again. Frowning, she stood still and studied her reflection. At just a few pence under £400 she would have thought the designer chiffon dress would transform even the plainest of women into a stunning model. But no, just like every other outfit she tried on, this just hung on her shapeless frame like a vastly over-priced sack.

Tracey hated special occasions. She was never much of a socialite and the pretentious carry-on just wound her up. She would use every excuse under the sun to try to slip away early.

Tonight's event was important though. It was one of the most prestigious nights in any performer's professional career and Tracey was intent on making a good impression. As she paraded once more in front of the mirror, her eye caught the reflection of the wall clock. 'Shit!' she exclaimed. The clock showed 7:35 and she had just 25 minutes to rush across town to the hotel function suite in Bloomsbury.

She grabbed up her clutch bag, threw a bolero around her shoulders and slipped into her stilettos.

Looking down at the six-inch heels, she shook her head; with the best will in the world, she'd never trek the mile and half journey in these!

She considered calling a cab, but she knew it would be a long wait at this time on a Saturday evening. She shoved her feet into a worn out pair of trainers, picked up her stilettos and sparkly clutch bag and rushed out of the door into the pouring rain.

Miranda D'Angelo was holding court in the banquet hall.

Journalists, dignitaries and fellow performers alike were all enjoying her anecdotes as they stood around drinking champagne. A podium on a small stage in the corner was being manoeuvred into position and the assembled guests turned their attention towards the stage.

'Good evening, ladies and gentlemen and welcome to the third annual event hosted by the MacMillan Quist production company. We have a lot to get through this evening, so without further ado I'd like to welcome on stage renowned playwright Gervais Macron.'

The room exploded with loud and enthusiastic applause.

A short man in a tuxedo walked onto the stage and took position on the podium. The room fell silent and – all but a small spot awashing the stage with milky white illumination – the lights dimmed

Gervais cleared his throat, but before he had a chance to speak the double doors at the back of the function room burst open and Tracey Tranter stepped in, dripping wet and dishevelled. With her wet hair hanging over her eyes she failed to notice a small table filled with empty glasses just inside the doorway and proceeded to walk into it, sending the vessels flying.

Gervais looked towards the rear of the room and all heads turned to follow his gaze.

There Tracey stood, silhouetted by the harsh light from the hallway outside, and never before had she so desperately wanted the ground to swallow her up more than at that moment. 'Oops!' she said with a nervous giggle as several staff holding hand brushes and dustpans came rushing towards the carnage.

Gervais gently tapped the microphone and clearing his throat again he announced, 'And the award for most dramatic entrance goes to…' He paused and waved his hand towards Tracey. 'Madam?' he prompted. The spotlight swung round and swathed Tracey in harsh white light.

'Tracey,' she replied nervously. 'Tracey Tranter.' The room erupted with laughter. Tracey stood there, her face crimson with embarrassment, as three men dropped to their knees around her to sweep up the broken glass.

As the evening continued, Tracey once again felt the nagging urge to make her excuses and leave. Her sole intention in blagging a ticket to this event was simply to press the flesh and make her face known; following her less than graceful entrance, it was certainly known now, but for none of the right reasons.

Since graduating from drama school, Tracey had not been short of work. No sooner did one turn end than another started, but everything she had been cast in thus far was amateur and low budget. Community theatres and fringe festivals were great fun, but she would never make a name for herself schlepping the boards in a dilapidated village hall.

Gervais Macron was one of the most respected playwrights of the last two decades. The opening night of his latest tragedy, "The Crows are Calling" in London's West End was less than a month away and although the coveted lead roles had already been cast, there were still a couple of openings for incidental characters. Tracey wanted a slice of this pie more than anything she'd ever wanted before.

She glanced around the room trying to locate Macron amongst the throng of people clad in tuxedos and ball gowns. As she looked over towards the buffet table her eyes locked on her quarry. He was a short man and very much hidden amongst the crowd that surrounded him, but there he was, the man that Tracey felt held her future in his small but perfectly manicured hands.

She nervously started to move towards him. Taking a deep breath, she desperately tried to shake the nerves and then purposely strode forwards.

Gervais looked up and saw Tracey approaching. He flashed her a warm and genuine smile and held out his hand. She reached out to take it and he bent to kiss the back of her hand. 'I do hope you're not planning a repeat performance,' he said with a cheeky grin, theatrically protecting the wine glass in his left hand.

'I'm really sorry. That was so embarrassing,' Tracey said coyly.

'Haha! Not at all, my dear girl,' Gervais replied, squeezing Tracey's arm reassuringly. 'I'm usually not too keen on being upstaged, but when one's show is stolen by someone as pretty as you... well, one is prepared to yield.'

Tracey tried hard to hide her embarrassment and graciously smiled at him. 'Thank you,' she said quietly.

'Now! What brings a natural beauty like you stumbling into this gathering of fakes and fraudsters?' Gervais asked, focussing his attention entirely on her.

'I'm an actress,' Tracey replied. 'I'm here with the Holloway Players,' she added.

Gervais raised one eyebrow curiously.

'Oh no!' Tracey exclaimed. 'Not the prison. We're a small am-dram group. You sponsored us last year.'

'Oh yes!' Gervais said with a smile. 'So are you appearing in anything right now?' he asked.

'No. I'm currently looking,' Tracey said, trying to hide the desperation in her voice.

'I have a new production and I'm sure there's a role for you in it somewhere.' Gervais pulled a business card from his jacket pocket. 'Call me tomorrow and we'll get you on the casting call.'

113

Tracey took the card and beamed a grateful smile. 'Thank you, Mr Macron, thank you *very* much!'

Gervais squeezed her arm again and with a friendly nod he returned the smile. 'Lovely to meet you, Miss Tranter.' As he walked away Tracey felt a wave of happiness; not only had she bagged a role in a Macron production, the man himself remembered her name!

Early the next morning Tracey awoke in a half dream. She lay for a moment as the ethereal world drifted away and her mind returned to lucidity. Then she yawned and flung back the duvet. Getting out of bed, she padded off to the bathroom and as she caught her reflection in the cabinet mirror, she smiled. Her dream was amazing. She had been standing alongside Gervais Macron, celebrated playwright and he had offered her a part in his new stage production… Wait… It *wasn't* a dream. He *did* offer her a part!

She hurried out of the bathroom and along the short hallway to the coathooks just inside the front door of her flat. Underneath her faux fur bolero was the sparkly clutch bag she'd had with her at the previous night's event.

She hurriedly opened it and fumbled inside. With a huge sigh of relief, she withdrew the business card from the bag and smiled. One side was black with a simple monogram and a picture of a quill pen and ink pot. As she turned it over, the reverse revealed the contact details; printed on a white background were the words

Gervais Macron LTD
Office: 0208 57485748
email: gmproductions@macron.com

Tracey hung the bag back on the hook and re-entered the bedroom. She picked up her mobile phone from the bedside cabinet and started to dial the number. She held the phone close to her ear and her heart started to pound in her chest. The ringing stopped and a voice on the other end said, 'Good morning, Gervais Macron Limited.'

Tracey was slightly thrown by the sound of a female voice. 'Oh, er... erm...'

'Can I help you?' the voice asked abruptly.

Composing herself, Tracey replied, 'Oh, yes, sorry. My name is Tracey Tranter. Could I speak to Gervais Macron please?'

The line fell silent for a moment and Tracey frowned.

'I'm sorry madam,' the voice said. 'Mr Macron doesn't take calls. Can I ask what it's regarding?'

'Er, yes. I spoke with him last night and he said to call today to arrange for a casting,' Tracey said, feeling slightly awkward.

'Ah. I see,' the voice replied. There was the sound of shuffling paper and the voice continued, 'Could you attend an audition in Wimbledon this afternoon at two-thirty?'

'Yes. Yes, of course,' Tracey replied enthusiastically.

'If you give me your email address I'll send the details over to you.'

Tracey gave the woman her address and the voice on the end of the line thanked her and said goodbye. Before Tracey had a chance to respond, the line went dead. She looked at the screen on her phone and it read **Call Ended**. She sighed and walked through into the kitchen to make breakfast.

Alex was sat up in bed looking at his mobile phone. His room was small and dark, and there was a thin shard of light beaming in through a crack in the blind. Around the walls were perfectly framed theatre handbills and posters. All of the matching frames proudly displayed promotional photos of Miranda D'Angelo. On a shelving unit beside the bed was an impressive collection of theatre programmes and a handful of DVDs, all featuring stage productions starring Miranda. Alex's membership to copious theatre appreciation clubs had afforded him access to premieres and special invitation-only events, as well as the opportunity to purchase exclusive merchandise, and he had lapped it up like an eager kid collecting football stickers.

On the shelf below, in almost stark contrast to the glitzy memorabilia above, was a collection of hunting magazines and books dedicated to shooting and various guns. Trophies adorned the bottom shelf, all effigies of little bronze and silver coloured men firing rifles.

Alex put down his phone and stretched. Two days into his summer leave and he was already missing the routine. His weekend had been better than average, seeing Miranda perform live on the Saturday and then spending a whole day at gun club on the Sunday. But on Monday he had sat in his boxers all day, flicking through various TV channels and settling on nothing in particular until the evening when his Deliveroo pizza arrived and he got engrossed in a "Fast and Furious" movie marathon until the early hours. Yesterday, when he had finally dragged himself out of bed, he'd spent most of the day cleaning his small flat and then wasted the evening playing "Call of Duty" on his Xbox.

Today he had vowed to do something more productive. He walked into his en-suite shower room and turned on the shower. He knew better than to step straight in; the water took an age to get hot and he hated nothing more than a cold shower. Kicking off his pyjama bottoms, he stepped in.

Alex's shower routine was precise and efficient. He would douse his hair, step back from the hose, apply shampoo, wash all over with a flannel and soap and then step back under the shower head to rinse away the suds. Maximum shower time for Alex never exceeded five minutes. His clothes were always folded neatly on the chest of drawers from the night before and, by the time he was dressed, his closely cropped hair was already dry. He never brushed his teeth until after breakfast and thought people that did so beforehand were clearly stupid.

As he poured himself a bowl of cornflakes, he flicked on a small TV in the kitchen. He rolled his eyes as the breakfast show came on and that sickly sweet couple he so despised chattered away inanely like a pair of annoying budgerigars. He picked up the remote and was about to change the channel when the male presenter announced, 'Please welcome onto the show Queen of the West End, Miranda D'Angelo!'

Alex turned his head so quickly that he almost lost his balance. How could he have forgotten that his beloved Miranda was being interviewed this morning?

He gazed lovingly at the TV screen, but his attention quickly returned to the task in hand as his feet suddenly felt cold and wet; he realised the milk had breached his cereal bowl and was now pouring onto his socks and across the kitchen floor. He put the bottle down on the side and, in a unusual show of nonchalance, he threw a tea towel over the milky puddle on the floor and stepped over closer to the television in a trance-like state.

He smiled as he watched Miranda breeze effortlessly through the interview. Every inane question the dozy presenters threw at her she answered with grace and intelligence and Alex swelled with pride.

The interview concluded with Miranda revealing she was leaving the show to attend rehearsals at the New Wimbledon Theatre for the upcoming West End show in which she was to be the leading lady. As he lead her off the set, the presenter who Alex despised leant passionately forward and kissed Miranda on the cheek. Alex's lip curled and he glared at the smarmy chat show host with abject hatred. His feelings of resentment soon subsided though as he recalled Miranda's parting sentence.

He bent over to remove his socks and strode back into the bathroom. Running the shower hose over his feet, he smiled as he planned his next move in his head.

He dried off his feet and squirted a generous helping of toothpaste onto his electric toothbrush. As the powered head rattled around in his mouth Alex looked at his reflection in the mirror. His closely cropped hair was neat and tidy, his face smooth and clean shaven. He was a handsome man with good features and an impressive stature, but there was a coldness in his eyes. He stared long and hard at himself and then delicately spat out the foamy toothpaste into the sink. He took up a handful of water and splashed it across his mouth before dabbing his face dry with a towel. Then, reaching for a bottle of cologne he sprayed a modest amount onto his neck and left the bathroom.

As he crossed the hallway heading for the bedroom, his eyes fell upon the tea towel on the kitchen floor. It was now damp, having soaked up the milk and he gently rolled it up and rinsed it out in the sink. He took a sheet of kitchen towel from the roll and knelt to spray the floor with antibacterial spray. Meticulously wiping the area, he then screwed the tissue into a ball and placed it in the bin.

Looking at his watch, he hurried into the bedroom where he put on a clean pair of socks and sat on the bed to tie his shoes. He slipped on his jacket and took one last look at himself in the long mirror fixed to the bedroom door, then without further delay he picked up his keys and left the flat. Destination: Wimbledon.

The train was late and Tracey was starting to panic. The overhead timetable wasn't working and she had no idea when or even *if* the train was coming. There were only three roles left to cast and if she turned up late, she'd be sure to miss out.

Pulling out her mobile phone, she opened the travel app to see if it could shed any light on the train's arrival.

She scrolled down to locate the station and it said: 1 MINUTE. She looked along the line. It was a clear day and she could see as far as where the line curved out of sight, but there was no sign of an approaching train. She looked back down at the phone screen and it simply read: DUE. Out of the corner of her eye she could see the LED sign above her head was flickering. Amber dots were fading in and out and they finally settled to reveal the words: STAND BACK. TRAIN APPROACHING. Underneath the bold message was a slightly smaller one, which said SHORT TRAIN: 3 CARRIAGES ONLY.

Tracey looked up to see the train snaking around the bend. 3 carriages only, she thought... It suddenly occurred to her that she was much too far along the platform and she started to walk quickly towards the other end, but as she hurried along one of her heels got caught between two paving slabs and broke away.

'Shit!' she exclaimed.

The train pulled up slowly alongside her but kept going. She took off both her shoes, picked up the broken heel and sprinted after it.

She reached the end door just in time and almost threw herself on board as a beeping noise sounded and the door slid shut.

Panting heavily Tracey slumped onto the one available seat in the carriage. She looked down at her tights, which were now laddered all the way from the feet upwards. Inspecting her right shoe left her in no doubt that the £350 half-price bargain from the outlet shop in Ashford had actually been a complete waste of money.

She sighed and checked her watch. There was still an hour and fifteen minutes until her audition and provided there were no more delays she should arrive in Wimbledon ten minutes early.

She sank back into the seat and lazily studied the advertisements pasted along the roof of the train.

Alex stepped off the bus and looked across the street. The golden Roman goddess atop the tower entrance to the New Wimbledon Theatre was reflecting the sun and the rays almost blinded him. He held his hand up to shield his eyes and made his way across the road towards the theatre. It was an unusually quiet day and he crossed the road with ease. He walked around the side of the theatre and towards the rear. Locating the stage door he took up position a few metres away. Looking around he was relieved to see that there was nobody else hanging about waiting for autographs.

There was a small convertible mini parked adjacent to the loading bay, but other than that the service area was empty. The faint sound of music was coming from inside the theatre. Alex cocked his ear to listen, but it was indecipherable. Distracted by the music, he failed to notice a car pulling into the service yard; its approach was almost silent as the electric engine was barely audible and it slowly turned to park.

The driver sounded the horn and Alex jumped. He stepped aside as the Land Rover with blacked out windows reversed to park beside the stage door.

The driver's door opened and a tall, stocky bald man stepped out. He cast a quick glance at Alex and then turned to open the rear door.

Alex watched intently as the driver stood back and a pair of long, shapely legs swung out.

As she stood up, Miranda locked eyes with Alex and for a moment he thought he might faint.

She turned away and as the driver shut the door Alex called out, 'Excuse me!'

Miranda and the driver continued towards the stage door. 'Er, Ms D'Angelo, I… I wondered whether you'd be kind enough to sign this.' Alex held out a photograph. In his other hand he was holding a silver marker pen.

Miranda stopped and turned to face him. Alex smiled at her and extended his hand a little further. She squinted at the photo and then looked up at Alex. He smiled again, hoping he wasn't starting to look desperate.

Miranda took a few steps towards him and stopped just short of his extended hands. She snatched the photograph from him and studied it.

Alex held out the pen and she swatted it away with the back of her right hand. It flew through the air and skidded across the tarmac before settling in the kerb.

Miranda, who beckoned her driver to come over and Alex stiffened defensively.

The driver stopped and Miranda clicked her fingers. 'Pen!' she snapped.

The driver pulled out a fine blue pen. She signed the photo with a quick flourish and handed the pen back to her driver. She then took hold of each corner and aggressively ripped the photo in half before thrusting it back towards Alex. 'Now scram, you strange little man,' she shrieked as she turned on her heels and hurried off to the stage door.

The driver tapped a code into the lock and the pair slipped inside, slamming the door behind them.

Alex stood for a moment trying to process what had just happened.

His idol was horrible. Truly horrible. He couldn't believe it. For as long as he could remember he had followed Miranda D'Angelo's career. He had bought every book, every DVD and CD, even that awful

Christmas cover album she'd recorded with Michael Ball... or Bublé... or was it Alfie Boe? It was so awful, he couldn't even remember. He'd been to every show and travelled the length and breadth of the country for her, and never in his wildest imagination had he thought the woman he'd idolised for so long could be so damned rude!

Alex slowly turned around and walked over to the marker pen lying at the kerb. He picked it up and slipped it into his inside pocket. Stepping out onto the main street, which had now become considerably busier, he walked solemnly back towards where he had alighted the bus. As he passed a litterbin, he posted the torn photograph through the slot and without any further hesitation carried on towards the bus stop.

As he walked along Russell Road with his head down, he failed to see a woman stepping out from a charity shop in front of him. The pair collided and Alex reached out his arms to prevent the woman from tumbling to the ground.

'I'm terribly sorry,' he said, as he helped steady her. 'I wasn't watching where I was going.'

The woman looked up at him gratefully. 'Oh, no, it was my fault, rushing around as always. The heel on my shoe broke off and I had to dash in here quickly to buy another pair.' She gestured down to her feet, clad in slightly lower black heels and then up at the shop front sign, which read HALFWAY HAVEN ANIMAL SANCTUARY. 'Three pounds fifty for a pair of shoes that'll probably last way longer than the ones I paid a hundred times more for!'

Alex smiled 'That's a bargain! I hope your day continues on such a positive note.' He smiled again and carried on up the street.

Tracey watched him walk away. 'What a lovely man,' she said quietly to herself. She looked at her watch and gasped. She had 2 minutes to get to the auditions.

She skittered along the street and whizzed round the bend. As she passed the litterbin she posted the disgraced designer shoes through the slot and the heel on the remaining good shoe got caught in the narrow opening. It fell to the ground and Tracey growled out loud. 'For flip's sake!' She picked it up and turned it sideways, gently depositing it through the slot, then hurried across the road towards the service yard to the backstage door.

There was a bell beside the entrance keypad and Tracey pressed it hard. 'Come on, come on,' she muttered under her breath.

The door opened and a man peered through the gap. 'Can I help you?' he asked.

'I'm Tracey Tranter. I'm here for an audition.'

The man looked at a list attached to a clipboard, following the names down with his pen. 'Tranter?' he asked.

'Yes, Tracey Tranter,' she replied.

The man continued to study the list.

'Mr Macron invited me along personally,' Tracey added.

The man looked up at her and his left eyebrow arched. 'Really?' he said sarcastically.

Tracey was starting to feel worried as the man raised his pen to the top of the list and started reading down again. The pen reached the bottom of the page and he looked up at her. 'There's no Tracey Tranter here.'

Tracey's face fell.

The man wrapped his fingers round the door and was about to close it when he said, 'Oh hang on! Silly me. There's another page underneath.' He flipped it back and there at the top, on its own, was Tracey's name.

She sighed with relief.

'You'd better come on in then,' the man said with an unconvincing smile.

As Alex climbed onto the bus, swiping his Oyster card, his eyes fell on the plastic wallet housing it and a wave of sadness washed over him. It was a limited edition plastic wallet that was part of a fan pack from one of the very first West End shows Miranda had appeared in. He'd kept it in its wrapper on a shelf for years until he had finally decided to use it. Whipping it out to scan his Oyster card always made him smile. Up until today at least.

He looked down the aisle of the lower deck and all the seats were full, so he made his way upstairs. As he reached the top of the stairs, the noise of teenagers at the back assailed his ears. He turned to face the front of the bus and all the seats were occupied, so he reluctantly took a seat near the back.

The noise was deafening and Alex reached into his inside pocket and pulled out a pair of earphones. He plugged them into his phone and started listening to music.

Turning the plastic wallet over in his fingers Alex reflected on what had happened less than half an hour earlier. As he held the wallet up to look at the small printed image of Miranda in a beautiful red velvet dress a grubby hand swept in from behind and whipped it out of his fingers.

Alex pulled the earphones from his ears and looked round at lightning speed.

A tall, lanky lad in a loose fitting green parka was walking back towards his cohorts on the back seat, waving the wallet in the air. 'Look at this poncy thing,' he said.

'Gissa look,' one of the other lads replied.

Tossing it across to his friend, the lad who'd taken the wallet turned to face Alex who was now standing. 'That your bird mate?' he asked mockingly.

Alex was silent as he stepped out from behind the seat and started to walk towards the lad laughing hysterically at his friend, who was now holding the wallet to his mouth and licking it with his full tongue lolling all over it.

Alex held out his hand and without any show of emotion he calmly said, 'Give me that back.'

'You what, bruv?' the lanky lad snapped back.

'I said give me back my wallet. Now!' Alex replied, this time with considerably more conviction.

The boy holding Alex's wallet stood up and it became apparent he was a lot bigger and more muscular than his streaky mate. He bowled along the aisle and stopped a couple of feet from Alex. He held out the wallet and said, "If you want it, take it.'

Alex stepped forward and reached out to retrieve his wallet. The thug threw it over his shoulder and it landed on the floor at the back of the bus. He laughed. 'Go on, fetch!' The lanky lad laughed out loud. 'Good one, Jay!'

All the passengers at the front of the bus had turned in their seats and were watching the drama unfold.

Alex fixed his eyes on the thug and glared at him. As the lad stared back at him Alex stepped forward and walked towards his wallet. The bulky thug stepped into the aisle to block his way, but in the blink of an eye Alex raised his left arm and deftly pushed him aside, forcing him down onto the seat.

The lanky lad stepped forward, but equally as fast Alex reached out with his right arm and grabbed the boy's fur hood. He twisted it several times around his hand pulling the boy closer towards him and held on, dragging him sideways as he bent to pick up his wallet. As he stood up straight, he unfurled the hood and pushed the lad down between the seats.

Jay had got to his feet and was once again blocking Alex's exit. Alex didn't stop and, as he approached, the lad stepped aside and let him pass.

Alex returned to his seat and the other passengers swivelled back to face the front. The bus continued its journey in an almost unearthly silence.

Tracey stepped out onto the boards. Except for a harsh white spotlight flooding the front of the stage, the lights were dim. There was a panel of five people sat in the front row of seats. One of them was Miranda and she sat cross-legged with a glass of gin resting on her knee.

Tracey gave her audition, an excerpt from "Phantom of the Opera", and the panel nodded appreciatively as she took a small bow and turned to leave the stage.

Backstage, a handful of actresses and actors were talking amongst themselves. Tracey stepped into the room and walked over to join them.

'How did it go?' a petite blonde girl asked.

'Okay I think,' Tracey replied.

They stood around making small talk until a tannoy fixed on the ceiling above their heads let out an ear-splitting screech and voice sounded: 'Could Carly Patterson please report to the stage.'

The blonde girl put down her drink. 'Ooh, that's me!' she exclaimed excitedly and hurried off towards the wings.

Tracey watched as one by one the other actors were called to the stage. She slowly strolled along the room admiring the framed black & white photographs adorning the walls. Each still had been taken in the theatre and depicted a scene from a show or a live music event. As she reached the far wall by the door, Tracey frowned at the slightly skewed photograph of a pantomime horse. She stretched out her right hand and lightly adjusted it with her thumb, slowly pushing it upwards. Stepping back, she tutted as she saw the picture was still crooked. She stepped forward and took the corner of the frame into her left hand. She was just about to readjust it when the tannoy burst into life and startled her. She jumped and her hand pushed the frame up. It unlatched from the hook on the wall and came crashing to the floor. She looked at it in dismay. The frame was split and the glass had completely shattered.

A voice sounded from the speaker. 'Could Tracey Trotter please return to the stage.'

'Tranter!' Tracey seethed, as she picked up the broken frame and placed it down on the table.

Retrieving the keys from his jacket pocket, Alex unlocked the front door of his flat and pushed it open. It jammed on a pile of mail inside on the doormat and wouldn't open any further. He calmly knelt down and hooked his arm around the door. Scooping up the mail he freed the door and stood up.

As he entered the flat his eyes fell upon a shrink-wrapped magazine on the top of the pile. "Theatre Today" was a monthly publication that Alex had subscribed to for the last eleven years. The feature on the front cover of this issue was a bold promotional spread for the upcoming Macron epic "The Crows are Calling" and an image of Miranda D'Angelo in a soft focus haze adorned most of the cover.

Alex sighed. The arrival of this magazine was usually a joyous occasion, but as he entered the kitchen he coolly dropped it onto the kitchen table along with the other mail.

Stepping back out into the hall, he removed his jacket and hung it onto a hook on the wall, then returned to the kitchen and opened the fridge. He reached in and pulled out a can of lager.

Alex wasn't the kind of man to drink alcohol in the middle of the day, but this was no ordinary day and in the absence of a tot of whiskey – a drink he refused to keep in the house – a lager would have to suffice. He sat down and took a small sip directly from the can.

Alex sifted through the mail, most of which was advertising leaflets. He looked curiously at a white envelope with a plastic window. Carefully splitting the top with his thumbnail, he opened it and pulled out a tri-folded piece of paper. He unfolded it and read a few lines. Picking up the envelope, he pulled out a thin piece of card. He turned it over and it shone back at him as the sunlight bounced off the gold emblem embossed onto it. It was a ticket for the Shaftesbury Theatre. Not just any ticket either; it was a VIP ticket for a box on opening night for "The Crows are Calling".

Alex stood up and lightly pressed his foot on the pedal bin. As the lid flipped open, he nonchalantly dropped the ticket into the bin.

As Tracey stepped out in front of the selection panel, she could feel her heart pounding. She willed herself to calm down and stood there silently whilst the assembly flicked through paperwork. They were clearly unaware of her arrival.

Tracey coughed softly and one of the men looked up over his spectacles towards the stage. 'Ah! Miss Trotter,' he announced.

The other four members looked up.

Tracey smiled awkwardly. 'It's Tranter.'

'Yes…,' the man replied, looking down as the paperwork on his lap.

Tracey scanned the faces. Seated at the end, Miranda D'Angelo was staring back at her. Tracey smiled and Miranda looked away.

'So. It says here that you have appeared in musical productions for community theatres.'

Tracey turned her attention to the bespectacled man. 'Yes,' she replied. 'I have been in a lot of musicals and pantomimes. I played Eva Perón last year and most recently I've been on tour with…'

The man held up his hand. 'Yes, yes, it's all here my dear.'

The man sat next to Miranda leaned forward and smiled at Tracey. 'We have had a lot of interest in this production. As I'm sure you'll appreciate the casting process for a show of such magnitude is stringent and the people we are looking for must be top of their game.'

Tracey nodded respectfully.

'Therefore,' the man continued, 'we are pleased to offer you a role in the production. A role which will require your full dedication.'

Tracey smiled. It was taking all of her strength to remain poised and contain her excitement.

'We have cast you as Kathleen Mahoney's understudy. This part is being played by Ms D'Angelo and you will be required to attend every rehearsal and learn the role as if it were your own.'

Miranda was still staring and it was starting to make Tracey feel a little uncomfortable. Suddenly she spoke. 'Make no mistake you are an understudy. This is my role and you are simply there as a stand-in.'

The other men on the panel looked awkwardly down at their paperwork as Miranda continued. 'You will form part of the ensemble and you will be billed as such. I am the leading lady and I…' she started to cough.

The man beside her offered her a bottle of water and she brushed his hand aside.

'*I*…' – Miranda cleared her throat – '*I* am Kathleen, it will be my face in the programme and on all the posters. As long as you remember that, we will all get along just fine.' With that, Miranda stood up and walked towards the door, stifling another cough as she sashayed off.

133

Alex was sat in an armchair in his small, yet perfectly organised lounge. The television was on in the corner of the room but the sound was muted. He was staring; not at anything in particular, just staring. His breathing was steady and the coldness in his eyes was etched with a distinct portrayal of despondency and sadness. He sat like this for a good hour, the world outside rushing by, going about its business without a moment's thought for the lost and miserable man suffering in silence inside number 39 Haltemprice House.

One could be forgiven for thinking Alex's vacant expression denoted absence of mind. It might even suggest that he had slipped into a distant world far away from the horrors of reality. But no, inside this quiet man's head a million thoughts were racing and suddenly, within the literal blink of an eye, they ceased. Alex breathed deeply and let out a big sigh.

He stood up and walked into the kitchen. Opening the fridge, he pulled out a bright green apple, crossed to the drawer set and opened the top one, from where he selected a small, sharp knife. Retrieving the theatre magazine, he removed the plastic wrap and took it to the bin. As the flip lid raised Alex could see the VIP ticket lying on top of the household refuse. He screwed the plastic up and tossed it in. Then he walked back to the lounge with the apple and magazine.

Sitting down, he placed the magazine on the arm of his chair, then deftly sliced a small piece of apple and popped it into his mouth. He looked down at the magazine cover on his right and with one swift movement he raised his right hand and plunged the knife down, sinking it straight through the middle of the magazine and into the sponge armrest beneath.

Leaving the knife protruding from magazine, he stood up, and walked out to the kitchen. He stepped on the pedal bin and reached in to pull out the ticket. He placed it on the kitchen worktop and walked over the window by the sink, and leaning with both hands on the windowsill he looked out to the street below.

He watched the people busily rushing about below him. He blinked several times as his mind erupted into a myriad of ideas and scenarios. His breathing became shallow and he nodded slowly. Then he turned to look at the ticket with its embossed emblem twinkling in the sunlight like a fine gold coin. He nodded again this time more decisively and marched off into his bedroom.

As Tracey stood on the platform at Paddington Station she scrolled through her mobile phone messages. Her brother Sam had sent several texts over the last couple of weeks and she felt a twinge of guilt for not replying sooner. The rehearsals for "The Crows" (as it had now affectionately been dubbed) had been gruelling and she had barely had a day to herself. In fact, this was her first Saturday off in a long time. A poor excuse, her brother would object. And maybe he was right.

Both she and Sam had left the family home at a young age. The village they'd grown up in was almost shut off from the modern world and they both knew that leaving for London was the only chance they had to make something of their lives. Sam was obsessed with money and the global economy and Tracey dreamt of becoming a West End star.

Their parents were happy in the village; they had both lived and worked there for their entire lives and had no interest in big towns and busy cities. May, their mother, ran the small village café and Bill, their father, had been the only mechanic in the area since his teenage years. It suited them.

Bill was disappointed that his son wasn't interested in learning the trade and he made it abundantly clear that he didn't approve of Tracey's "fanciful daydreaming", but the family remained close and there was no doubt in either of the sibling's minds that they were both loved.

Sam's texts weren't unusual. He hardly ever picked up the phone to speak and if he did it was usually to have a dig. This time around however, Tracey conceded that her brother had good reason to nag. The pair took it in turns to visit their parents on alternate weekends, but over the last few months, wrapped up in her desperation to find a decent role in a professional production, Tracey had let her duties slide. Sam had been reasonable at first, but this week's texts hit a nerve and the realisation that her mother's health was deteriorating prompted Tracey to make the effort.

As the train drew to a halt, Tracey hopped on board and took a seat. She looked up at the map and seeing the short journey of six stops laid out before her eyes made her feel even more guilty.

She opened her phone and started to tap out a reply to her brother.

Miranda lay face down with her arms splayed at her side. Her head was wedged and her face slightly contorted.

'Is that okay for you?' a voice enquired.

'Yes, lovely,' Miranda mumbled through the padded hole in the massage bench.

A spa day was just what the doctor ordered. Miranda had been feeling inordinately tired the last few days and despite her protestations to the contrary she secretly knew that a few days rest before opening night were much needed. The idyllic five star resort tucked away in the Hertfordshire countryside was Miranda's favourite bolthole and the service was second to none.

After the massage she retreated to her private cabin. Inside was a king size four-poster bed, a comfy chair facing a modest sized television and a dressing table with a large mirror.

Sprawled across the top of the dressing table was an array of bottles and packets. Miranda left nothing to chance and wherever she went, her medicines and therapies went with her. She poured a sticky liquid into a small dispenser and tipping back her head she swallowed it in one gulp. She looked at herself in the mirror. She had no makeup on and she stared long and hard at the gaunt face peering back at her. She breathed in deeply and suddenly started to cough. It was a dry cough and it made her eyes water. She quickly reached for the bottle of linctus and poured herself another helping. She swallowed and relaxed as the warm liquid trickled down her throat.

With a heavy sigh she slumped into the armchair and reached for the TV remote. She flicked through channels and settled on an old black and white movie, half watching it until she fell asleep in the chair.

Tracey stepped down from the train and walked along the short platform to the exit. She breathed in deeply, inhaling the fresh air she had never really appreciated until the time she'd upped sticks and moved to London. She glanced at her watch and smiled; she had made good time and knowing her mother would still be working in the café she decided to go straight there and surprise her.

Tracey pushed open the door to the café and a little bell jangled. Inside there were three round tables and a small counter with a large glass refrigerator beside it containing drinks.

'I won't be a minute,' a voice rang out from the kitchen.

Tracey walked towards the counter and was met by a lady wearing an apron and hairnet. She was carrying a glass cake stand containing a chocolate cake.

'Hello, Tracey love,' the woman said with a smile.

'Hi, Laura. How are you doing?' Tracey asked.

Laura put down the cake stand and stepped out to give Tracey a hug. 'I'm fine, love, what about you?'

Tracey smiled. 'Yeah, all good.' She craned her neck to look around the doorframe into the kitchen. 'Where's Mum?' she asked.

'Oh she's not been in for weeks. Her legs have been really bad lately and I know she's finding it a struggle.' Laura handed Tracey a slice of cake on a small plate. 'Would you like a cup of tea, love?'

Tracey smiled. 'Could I have a takeaway? I'm going to make my way over to the house,' she said, putting the plate down on the glass topped counter.

'Of course, love. Give me that cake, I'll wrap it up for you.'

Tracey pushed the plate along to Laura, who picked it up and slipped it into a white paper bag. ''Scuse fingers,' she said with a smile. She handed the paper bag and a lidded cardboard cup to Tracey. 'Give my love to your mum,' she said as Tracey rummaged around her handbag.

'I will,' she replied as she unzipped her purse. She looked up at Laura.

'You can put that away, love. It's on the house.'

Tracey smiled as Laura turned around and hurried back into the kitchen.

Tracey stepped out into the street and looked up at the bright blue sky. The sun was blazing and there wasn't a single cloud in sight. She looked across the road towards a line of trees and started to cross.

139

There was a pathway leading through the woodlands. It was a little overgrown, but Tracey had fond memories of time spent in the woods and every opportunity she had she would always walk that way to her parents' house.

The path was very bumpy; the hardened mud was in deep divots caused by horses during the wetter months. Tracey found the terrain hard going and was beginning to wish she had actually taken the road. Her legs started to ache and she decided that now was a good time to sit down and have her tea. She looked around for a log to sit on, but other than brambles and a deep carpet of fern there was nothing suitable in sight. Up ahead of her, she could see a clearing in the bushes, so she plodded on. The path veered slightly to the right and Tracey could see a few fallen tree branches on the ground. She made her way towards them and was surprised how dark it had become as the shadows of the tall trees and fulsome bushes shrouded her.

She selected a comfortable looking log and went to sit down, but before her bottom touched the wood she looked through a small parting in the bushes and was dazzled by an almost ethereal light that swathed the small copse beyond.

Intrigued, she walked towards it and slipped through the parting in the bushes. There in front of her was an old well. The cobblestone wall of the structure looked as if it would be a much more comfortable seat where she could rest her feet and tuck into her tea and cake.

Brushing the ivy aside, Tracey gently perched on the wall.

She flipped the lid from her cup and it tumbled lightly down into the well. 'Oops!' Tracey exclaimed as she watched it flutter down out of sight.

She took a sip of her tea and winched as the hot liquid entered her mouth. She carefully put the cup down and pulled out the slice of chocolate cake. 'Mmmm, amazing!' she said aloud as crumbs sprinkled from her mouth.

The trees surrounding the copse gently waved in the light breeze, casting strange shadows across the grass. Tracey did a double take as one of the shadows extended towards her. For a moment the dark shapes looked like a long pair of twisted hands reaching out to grab her.

Finishing her cake, she dabbed at her mouth with a napkin and picked up her tea. Then she stood up and started to walk around the well.

The whole area in this oasis was beautifully kept. Wild flowers bordered the copse and the grass was neat and free from weeds. The well itself was ancient and in remarkable condition for its age. Other than the creeping ivy snaking around the roof and a small sign, which had fallen to the ground, it was clean and in a perfect state of repair. Tracey bent to pick up the sign. As she turned it over, woodlice fell off the underside and scurried away. Slightly disgusted, she stepped back. 'Urghh,' she cried.

Engraved into the wood, Tracey could just make out the words **MAKE A WISH**. She chuckled to herself. 'Where would I start?' She placed the sign on the wall of the well. 'Oh, what the hell?' she said, reaching into her bag. She opened her purse and pulled out a pound coin. Stepping up to the opening she dropped the coin in and thought for a moment. She wasn't a superstitious person, but she knew that wording a wish correctly was important; she must choose her words carefully. She took a deep breath and called down quietly into the chasm, 'I wish just for once I'd be given the leading part in a West End show.' She stood waiting for a moment. She wasn't sure why or what she was expecting, but it felt a little rude to make a wish and just stroll off.

She picked up her cup and looked down into the blackness. 'Thank you,' she called out before walking off out of the copse and back towards the path.

Alex sat at his desk. It had been a long week and although immersing himself in his work had been a great distraction from his other woes, every evening as his colleagues left and the office fell silent he felt a certain dread about having to go home to his empty flat.

He shut down his computer and leaned back in his chair. The distant hum of a vacuum cleaner was echoing along the corridors of the civic building.

A shadow fell over the desk and Alex turned to see his manager David stood beside him. 'Come on lad, haven't you got a home to go to?' he said warmly.

Alex sat forward and reached under the desk for his satchel. He stood up and smiled politely. 'Good night, boss,' he said wearily.

David watched Alex slowly plod towards the exit. 'Is everything okay, lad?' he called out.

'Yeah, fine,' Alex called back before reaching for the door and trudging off out of the office and down the stairs.

David watched him leave, his face etched with concern. He turned to look at Alex's desk. It was spotlessly tidy; there was nothing on the surface except for the computer monitor and keyboard. He reached down and slid open the top drawer. All of the stationary was arranged in neat compartments. He opened the bottom drawer and it was as meticulously organised as the other. He pushed it shut and walked towards the door. Flicking off the lights, he locked up and made his way down the stairs whistling as he went.

The hustle and bustle back stage was a mixture of nerves and excitement. Rehearsals over the past fortnight had been relentless and although the cast and crew were confident that everything was running as smoothly as possible there was still that nagging doubt. The communal canteen was alive with the hubbub of voices, but along the various corridors it was mostly silent as the cast were relaxing behind closed doors in the dressing rooms.

From behind the door of dressing room number one, Miranda lay slumped on a chaise lounge with a slice of cucumber over each eye. There was a light tapping on the door and Miranda sighed. Removing the cucumber she called out hoarsely, 'Enter!'

The door slowly opened and a face appeared around it. 'Miranda darling, how lovely to see you.'

Miranda stood up and extended her hand. 'Gervais. It's an honour.'

He took her hand and lightly kissed the back of it. 'The honour is all mine.'

'Do come in,' Miranda beckoned.

Gervais stepped in and she closed the door behind him. His eyes fell upon a dummy head on the dressing table with an ornate wig on top; the fiery red hairpiece had black roses fed into it and a black mesh veil hung from the front. He looked around the small room and smiled as he noticed a black silk gown hanging in the corner. 'The costume department have excelled themselves.'

Miranda smiled weakly. She had her hand on the back of the chair and appeared quite unsteady.

'Is everything okay, my love?' Gervais asked with a note of concern.

Miranda picked up a piece of paper from the dressing table and started to fan herself with it. 'Yes,' she croaked 'I'm just a bit hot.'

Her forehead was clammy and Gervais couldn't help noticing that she was clearly sweating. He turned to face the outside wall. There was a small window up high near the ceiling and it had bars across it. 'That's not much use!' he exclaimed. He stepped towards Miranda and gently pulled out the chair. Taking her elbow he guided her into the seat. 'Sit there, my love. I'll get you a glass of water.'

Gervais rushed off leaving Miranda flopped in the seat, feverish and listless.

Alex stood before the full-length mirror attached to the back of his bedroom door. Dressed in a three-piece tuxedo, he adjusted the cummerbund before fastening up his jacket. He patted the sides and pulled at the hem whilst checking his reflection from every angle. His shoes shone back up at him as he turned them from side to side.

There was a gentle toot from outside and Alex walked over to the window. Acknowledging the driver with a small wave, Alex picked up the ticket from the kitchen worktop and made his way out of the flat and downstairs to the awaiting taxi.

Backstage at The Shaftesbury Theatre, there was a unmistakable air of uncertainty. A first aid call had been actioned and there was a lot of activity surrounding the dressing room area. Rumours were circulating, but with the area cordoned off nobody could be sure what was actually going on.

With less than half an hour until curtain up the stage manager had asked for all cast and crew to report to the canteen. Shuffling along the narrow corridors, the actors, stagehands and back house crew were mumbling to each other as they headed for the canteen. As they filtered through the doorway, Tracey let the crowd settle before taking up a position at the back of the room. Her attention was drawn to the unmistakable blue lights of an emergency vehicle in the car park outside. She put her hands to the glass and could see a stretcher being loaded in to the back of an ambulance.

A voice sounded from across the room and Tracey turned to face the front. 'Thank you all for coming. I will make this brief as time is not our friend right now.' The man speaking was Gavin Price, the stage manager. 'Unfortunately a member of our cast has been taken ill suddenly so we need to make a few adjustments. An official statement will be made at the end of tonight's performance, so I would ask you not to speak to anyone regarding this unprecedented line up change.'

Tracey was looking around the room. In a quick headcount she had managed to locate the majority of the crew, but the most notable absentee was Miranda.

'I regret to inform you that our leading lady, Ms D'Angelo has been taken ill,' Gavin continued. 'We are yet to ascertain the severity of her condition, but it has been confirmed that she will not be appearing in tonight's performance. Therefore...' – Gavin stopped to read from a clipboard – '...could Tracey Tranter from the ensemble please stay behind after this meeting. Everything else in the production will remain the same other than the ensemble in acts two and six, which will now be reduced to seven cast members with very minor adjustments to the lighting positions in respect of this. Do we have any questions?'

The room fell silent.

'Okay. Well thank you for coming and remember the show must go on. This is opening night and we have a very special audience tonight so go out there and give it your best.'

The canteen quickly emptied as everyone except Tracey made their way out of the room.

'Hi,. I'm Tracey,' she announced quietly.

'Well, my dear, you are now Kathleen Mahoney. Are you prepared?' Gavin asked

'Yes, sir, I'm prepared.'

Well, get yourself to dressing room one and go out there and knock 'em dead!'

Tracey smiled. 'Yes, sir.' With that she scuttled off out of the canteen and along the rabbit warren like network of corridors to the dressing room.

In the foyer the concierge stood by a red rope barrier with his perfectly white gloved hands crossed in front of him. The door staff were poised and the crown gathered on the steps outside were eager to enter the theatre. As the clock reached 7:00pm the doors opened in unison and the staff took position to check tickets. A separate door at the end opened and the doorman lifted out a sign with a placard, which read VIP Tickets.

Alex joined the queue at the end. As the audience slowly approached the door staff, tickets in hand, Alex watched with interest as they opened their handbags and turned out their pockets before being granted entry. He turned to face the queue directly in front of him; it was moving through a lot quicker than the general admissions.

As he approached the man on the door, Alex reached into his inside pocket. The doorman watched as he withdrew his hand and showed him his ticket. With a smile the doorman waved Alex inside, where he was greeted at the stairwell by an older gentleman in a red suit and hat. Alex held out his ticket and the man quickly examined it. 'Good evening, sir, would you like to follow me?'

Alex nodded and followed the man through the doorway and up the stairs to the private box.

The theatre filled at a steady pace and the auditorium was humming with the sound of hundreds of voices. Alex looked at the red velvet seats below quickly becoming occupied one by one. The lights on the ceiling dimmed and the stragglers hurried into their seats as the lamps along the walls also went out and the theatre was plunged into darkness.

The orchestra started to play and the drapes slowly opened, revealing a stage set with a Victorian carriage and a single lamppost. Dry ice was rising from the floor of the stage and dissipating like fog in the harsh light of the spotlight beaming onto the right side of the stage.

A man appeared dressed in a top hat and long black overcoat. As he strolled across the stage the audience burst into rapturous applause. He stopped in the centre of the stage and launched into a song.

Alex watched intently, leaning on the handrail as his eyes followed the man's movements. He looked across the auditorium to the box opposite. The light obscured his view, but he could just make out several silhouetted people sat back in their seats attentively watching the show. He returned his attention to the stage.

Back in the dressing room, Tracey was applying her makeup. As she looked into the mirror she giggled. She was here in Miranda's dressing room, wearing Miranda's gown and was she just about to put on Miranda's wig and step out onto the stage for a West End premiere show in front of a full house. She felt as if all her wishes had come true. She giggled again as she recalled her lunch break at the old well in Blechnum woods and how, after making her wish, she'd carried on to her parents' home where she had endured another lecture from her less than supportive father, who had insisted she was wasting her time bumming around London trying to become an actress. If only he could see her now, she thought.

A light crackled on above the door and an announcement from a small speaker on the dressing table said, 'Five minutes to stage left.'

Tracey dabbed at her lips with her finger and checked her appearance in the mirror. She reached for the wig and positioned it on her head. Carefully adjusting it, she tugged it into place and lowered the veil. Then, taking one last look in the mirror, she smiled and made her way towards the stage.

Now in act three, the set had been changed and with dry ice swathing the boards, the tops of gravestones could only just be seen amongst the dense fog. A solemn bell sounded and four men walked onto the stage carrying a coffin. The sound of cawing echoed around the auditorium and the lights dipped at the back of the stage to reveal several animatronic crows perched on a fence. The men placed the coffin down and stepped back as a man dressed in a priest's cassock walked onto the stage followed by a woman in a long black gown and veil. The woman knelt by the coffin and a piano started to play a haunting melody. The woman started to sing as the spotlight fell on her kneeling on the ground.

Alex leant forward.

The woman's voice was beautiful and built to a crescendo as the coffin started to drop below. The audience were wiping tears from their cheeks, the ladies dabbing at their eyes with handkerchiefs and the men swallowing hard trying to hide their emotion.

Alex reached into his inside pocket.

As the coffin disappeared out of sight, the priest stepped forward and burst into a baritone voice: 'Kathleen, Kathleen, please don't cry...' He held out his hands and helped her up.

Pushing him aside, and as she moved to the centre of the stage the spotlight followed her.

The audience were silent, all eyes on Kathleen.

The music slowly faded and then the silence was abruptly shattered by a loud bang, which echoed around the theatre.

Kathleen fell to the ground and the audience gasped. The priest stood there aghast.

A single clap erupted from the audience as others joined in building up to a round of applause.

A man ran out onto the stage. It was Gavin Price. He knelt beside Tracey and screamed out, 'She's been shot!'

He looked up into the single box above the left of the stage where a faint plume of smoke shimmered in the light. As he stared down at Tracey's lifeless body a small puddle of dark blood pooled around her head and trickled across the stage.

WHO WANTS TO LIVE FOREVER?

Tim Greaves

Being as I am someone who has specialised exclusively in works of fiction you may find what follows incredible to the point of disbelief.

So strange is it that I can scarcely believe it myself, so I have no real expectation that you will. However, I assure you, hand on heart, every word of this account is true.

Although I shall endeavour to stay focussed, I hope you'll bear with me if some of it seems a little... disconnected. But I'm so very tired, you see.

Why would I not wait until my mind is a little clearer, you might well be wondering. The thing is, I have no choice but to get this committed to paper tonight. Because if things go the way I intend them to, these will be the last words I shall write.

If it hadn't been for my dear, beloved Donna, I doubt very much you'd be reading them anyway. If Donna hadn't done what she did...

But wait, please forgive me, I'm getting ahead of myself.

For the benefit of those reading who may not be familiar with me – and, without wishing to appear immodest, I doubt that there will be many who aren't – I suppose I should introduce myself.

My name is Michael Chalvington.

Does that ring any bells?

Yes, that's correct, *the* Michael Chalvington, celebrated author of the Tobias Fulton detective series, which to date comprises 25 full length adventures – one of which is currently awaiting publication – and four short story compendiums, all translated into 72 languages and having sold over 970 million copies around the globe. Oh, and although they were less worthy offerings in my opinion, I suppose I ought to mention the handful of *very* short stories, barely more than four or five pages each, commissioned exclusively by upmarket magazines. (Please excuse me again, I forget exactly how many there were.)

Now I look at that all that written down before me, it's rather impressive, isn't it? Not bad for a man who once struggled to find a publisher prepared to even look at the first Fulton novel, "Stolen Midnight".

But enough of the ego-stroking. Looking at the bigger picture, none of it matters. You know who I am, and if you don't... well, that doesn't matter either really. It's the story I have to tell that you're here for.

Where to begin then?

There's no time for us...

"I'm sorry, I didn't have time."

How often have you had someone say that to you? Usually it's little more than a procrastinative excuse; a convenient string of words uttered by someone who has no real interest or intention in doing whatever it was they've promised – and resolutely *failed* – to do. Our daily lives overspill with so much minutiae jostling for attention, yet it's often the things that matter the most that get pushed aside.

"He has all the time in the world."

Alan Young, playing Rod Taylor's loyal friend in "The Time Machine" (one of my favourite films, incidentally) said it. And James Bond said the same thing, or a minor variation thereof. Twice. Louis Armstrong sang about it and Iggy Pop, of all people, covered it; remarkably well too, I'd concede, although it will never be anything more than an imitation. Whether Louis or Iggy did it best was an ongoing but genial point of contention between Donna and I that was never resolved.

I cannot help but smile now, remembering how animated she would become when stating her case. She was firmly in camp Iggy.

But to return to the point, none of us really have the time that we think we do. Life is short and our time on this planet is finite. Nobody is more aware of the ramifications of daring to think otherwise than I.

For as long as I can remember, I've had a problem with the idea of living an unremarkable life; to pass on without having achieved something, *anything* of worth that I might be remembered for. It perturbs me that when I die that vast jumble of moments unique to my life – moments that no-one else has experienced and never could have, because they're distinctively *mine* – will be snuffed out in an instant. The words I've spoken, the people I've known, the places I've been to, the things I've seen and done, the infinitesimal personal feelings of pride and shame, overwhelming love and intense hatred, confidence and fear, awe and loathing, happiness, sadness, satisfaction, arousal, jealousy, anger... All gone. Forever.

My Dad, God rest his soul, worked hard in what at best one could only refer to as a bill-paying job, but he provided well for his family; including my mother, there were six of us. Dad had his passions and interests, but he never translated them into anything that left an indelible mark.

How many of us are guilty of that?

Of course, our friends and our loved ones remember us when we're gone, but they're relatively few in number. There may be one or two people whose lives we've touched in some way who might think of us on occasion: "Oh yes," they'll say, "I think I remember him." But when they're all gone, so too is the memory of us.

And so it is that we die for a second time.

They say that figuratively speaking most people live on after death until the very last person who remembers them is laid to rest beneath the earth. And then that memory is buried along with them. They cease to have existed.

Dad passed away when I was young, but aside from myself – each of my siblings have now passed on, taking the memory of Dad to the grave with them – all that remains to show he was ever even here is a name engraved on a cuboid granite memorial vase in an overgrown corner of a tiny churchyard in Stoke Poges. Tended to by loved ones until they are no longer able, perhaps, but ultimately to be forgotten until the ravages

157

of countless storms have battered the name into submissive illegibility.

That's not how *I* wanted to end up. I wanted to be remembered by millions of people, whether they knew me or not.

Just consider for a moment how many people have trodden this planet since the beginning of time; the official estimate is something in the region of 107 *billion.* Mind-boggling, isn't it? Yet how many of them are remembered?

Even fame, or infamy, has a shelf life, although there are notable exceptions.

Who among you, old or young, hasn't heard of Charlie Chaplin, Lon Chaney, Louise Brooks or Babe Ruth? Few I would imagine. But, regardless of the fact they all had immense celebrity stature in the arenas of cinema and sport, I would posit that few among you will know the names Florence Lawrence, Norma Talmadge, Colleen Moore, Satchel Paige or "Red" Grange.

The same goes for the great writers that litter history. Could you say with any certainty what Edith Wharton, Upton Sinclair or Zane Grey wrote? If you could, well done. I'm impressed. Yet ask anyone who William Shakespeare, Sir Arthur Conan Doyle and Jules Verne were and they would know without a doubt.

They are the exceptions, and I wanted so desperately to be a part of that exclusive club.

The problem for me was the time it would take to make that indelible mark. For time was a luxury I didn't have.

At the age of 27 I was diagnosed with a rare hereditary condition known as Huntington's disease. I had never even heard of it before. For Huntington's there is no cure. It is fatal. Less than one in every 10,000 people get it, but I was one of them.

So you see, it's so important that everyone use what is gifted them wisely.

Because for some of us there really is no time.

There's no place for us...

I first encountered Donna Cavarro at a book signing.

I don't mean that to sound more grandiose than it actually was, but the simple fact is that was where we met.

I was sitting at a small table at the annual South Kensington book fair, with about a hundred copies of "Stolen Midnight" arranged in neat piles in front of me. It was, as I mentioned earlier, the first of the Tobias Fulton adventures.

I'd been reluctant to attend the fair – self-promotion was never my forte – but under the assurance of Ralph Banister that the event would be well attended I had caved in and we'd booked a shared dealers' table. (Oh, Ralph, I must tell you, was my oldest friend. The plan was that he would be selling his own book – a science fiction abomination which I had read and, without wishing to sound haughty, really wasn't very good – and I would be selling mine.) Ralph pulled out at the eleventh hour when he was seconded to make up a golf foursome at the Carns Hall Estate course near Portchester. I confess I felt somewhat abandoned, but in spite of my initial doubts, I was uncharacteristically optimistic about the day ahead, so I went along anyway.

After all, I had a lot of books to sell.

"Stolen Midnight" was a story that had been rattling around in my head for some time before I actually started to write it. It was a devilishly clever variation on the usual "private eye solves a serpentine mystery" format. When it was finished I was over the moon with the results and absolutely convinced I would have a hit on my hands.

How incredibly naïve I was back then.

Having spent almost two years hawking it around more publishers than I care to remember, I had failed to find one that was even remotely interested. Those who did actually deign to read it and reply were largely polite, their standard brush-off flimflam amounting to "it's good, but it's not for us". Most, I can tell you, did *not* reply.

I don't mind admitting that at the time I was crestfallen. But I won't pretend that even now, all these years later, it doesn't tickle me to think about how those short-sighted acquisitions agents dismissed my work so offhandedly, and how they must have kicked themselves later.

In any event, desperate that my book should be seen – I had, after all, poured almost a year of my life into writing it – I took the self-publishing route. Disaster! I was taken in by one of those unremunerative deals where you pay out of your own pocket to have your book printed. I'm too embarrassed to tell you how much the outlay was, suffice to say that it was not insubstantial.

What hadn't occurred to me, fool that I am, was how I would actually sell the things. That sounds ridiculous now, but I simply hadn't thought it through. Acting upon my impulses without due consideration of the outcome is one of my many foibles.

So there they sat, eight large boxes of paperback books taking up floor space in my spare room, and I hadn't a clue what to do with them.

But I'm digressing too much.

When an author starts talking about his work, he really can become the most frightful bore. I count myself as no exception.

I'm supposed to be telling you about Donna.

Now, where was I?

Oh yes, sitting behind a table at the book fair, which, while undeniably well attended by potential buyers, hadn't afforded me the sale of a single copy of "Stolen Midnight". I cannot tell you how dejected I was feeling.

I had my head buried in a book – not my own, I should hasten to add, I'm not quite *that* egotistical – and I didn't hear the woman approach.

'Hello.'

The soft voice gave me a little start and I dropped my book.

I looked up to see who had spoken.

Years may have passed since then, but I can describe the woman standing before me that day as precisely as if she were here with me right now.

She was what I suppose could best be described as petite. I'm not tall, but even in the flat-soled shoes on her feet she must have been more than two inches shorter than me.

She was wearing a white summer dress, cut not particularly low, but sufficiently so as to reveal a tantalising glimpse of the crevice between her breasts. The dress was dappled with tiny clusters of pink strawberries and it fell just above the knee.

She wore no make-up, but her pale, unblemished face had no need for it. Beneath perfectly arched eyebrows, her sapphire blue eyes sparkled at me. Heart-shaped vermilion lips, sculpted cheekbones and a pretty nose – ever so slightly upturned, tacitly inviting one to plant a soft kiss upon it – were framed by hair the colour of a golden sunrise, which tumbled around her shoulders in tight, natural curls.

Until that moment I would have scoffed at the frankly absurd notion of love at first sight. But that day my scepticism was well and truly challenged. She was without question was the most beautiful woman I had ever seen.

For a moment words failed me. I just sat there staring at her.

Her mouth formed into a smile at my evident discombobulation and she extended a slender hand. The perfectly manicured fingernails were coated in the palest blue varnish. 'My name's Donna. Donna Cavarro.'

I took her hand in mine. The softness and coolness of her skin was thrilling. 'Michael Chalvington.'

She laughed. Not mockingly, but full of warmth. 'I know.'

'You do?'

She pointed to the pile of books in front of me, the covers of which, naturally enough, bore my name. 'I assume this is your book?'

'It is.' As you may have noticed, I was still struggling to string more than two coherent words together.

I hadn't seen that she was clutching a book of her own. She held it up. 'This is mine.'

It was a children's storybook. I looked at the bold green title on the cover: The Very Wicked Frog. Her name was printed beneath it.

'My very first book.' She laughed. 'And probably my last. This is the first time I've done one of these things. I only picked up my stock from the printer yesterday. I've got a stall over there.' She gestured over her shoulder. 'I've been here all day and I haven't sold a single copy.' She laughed again. It was like the sound of fluttering angels' wings.

(Forgive me, I'm beginning to sound farcically poetic. That's the writer in me. Obviously her laugh wasn't *really* like that. I mean I haven't the faintest idea what fluttering angels' wings might even sound like. The thing is, as you can probably tell, I was smitten.)

'Oh dear, that's not good,' I said, trying to sound sympathetic, but not entirely succeeding. I was all too familiar with the despondency born of a failure to interest others in one's book.

'Yes, a little disheartening,' she said.

I once again found myself at a loss for words. After a few seconds of awkward silence she said, 'I've been watching you. You haven't sold anything either.'

For a fleeting moment I felt irrationally inadequate. 'No, I haven't.' I sighed. 'To be honest I didn't really want to come today in the first place. But now I'm rather glad I did.'

Don't laugh. I knew it was a corny line, but it's the best I could summon on the spur of the moment. Which isn't to suggest I'd have been able to come up with anything better if I'd had a week to think about it. I've always envied those men who seem to be able to capture a woman's attention effortlessly. I've never been one of them.

Donna smiled down at me. 'How much longer are you going to give it?'

'Excuse me?'

'Until you pack up and head home.'

I looked about me. The footfall had definitely eased off in the past half hour. 'I don't really know. I mean, I've got nowhere to be. I was thinking I'd sit it out, but...'

'I've certainly had enough. What do you say we both pack up now and go find somewhere to get a bite to eat. This is no place for the likes of us. We deserve better.'

I paused, only for a moment, but unfortunately long enough to embarrass her.

The pale skin on her cheeks blushed the most delicate shade of pink. 'I'm sorry, that was awfully forward of me. We only met 30 seconds ago and here I am asking you...' She fanned her face with her hand. 'And now I'm getting all flustered. Sorry.'

'No, *I'm* sorry. I mean... well, I've never been asked out on a date before.'

She smiled again, her embarrassment gone. She was utterly enchanting. 'Well, it's hardly a date. But if you'd like to join me... My treat.'

'I'd be delighted to.'

I hadn't sold a single book that day. But I didn't care. I had met Donna Cavarro and little did I know that she would not only save my life, she would change it forever.

We enjoyed a pleasant meal in a small bistro near the venue that was hosting the book fair. Two wannabe writers, sharing our stories and getting to know one another.

At the end of the evening we exchanged phone numbers, but I admit that as we parted company I never really expected to hear from her again.

I really should have more self-assurance, for two days later the phone rang and it was Donna.

She was over the moon. She'd just sold her first copy of "The Very Wicked Frog" and she wanted to share her excitement with me. I knew how she felt. I recalled the first sale that I ever made, that indescribable feeling of elation when a total stranger takes a blind chance on something *you've* written. You want to actually *be* there when they read it, a fly on the wall, watching to see how they react; if they're thrilled in the right places, if they smile as you hope they will at all the little humorous bits.

I asked Donna to accompany me to dinner to celebrate. My treat this time, of course. To my delight she accepted.

One year and seven days later Donna Cavarro said the words "I do" and became Mrs Donna Chalvington. I felt like the luckiest man on the face of the planet and it was without question the happiest day of my life, second to none.

We honeymooned in Paris; the city of love as it's known. I can certainly see why.

Neither of us had any interest in frequenting the familiar tourist haunts. Instead we spent the days exploring the hidden delights of the back streets and taking light luncheons in the most off the beaten track cafeterias that we could find, where we dined on flamiche and cassoulet and ratatouille, tarte tatin and apple cranberry galette and the lightest chocolate mousse imaginable; all washed down with the most delicious wines I've ever tasted.

Our nights were spent making love into the small hours, then drifting off to sleep in the toasty euphoria of post-coital bliss.

Nine months later, well eight months, three weeks and four days to be precise –

Slow down now. Please don't start second guessing what I'm going to say. You've read the clichéd expression "nine months later" and you've jumped to conclusions. I know what you're thinking. In your position I probably would be too. I only wish what I'm about to tell was *that* and not what it actually was.

– As I was about to say, eight months, three weeks and four days later I was diagnosed with Huntington's.

Prognosis: Terminal.

I shall spare you the details of the symptoms of this cruel disease. If you're interested you can look them up on the internet, or better yet take the traditional route and use a book.

After my diagnosis I slipped into a very dark funk. The thing that worried me most was the impending degenerative impact the condition would have on my cognitive faculties, and I became increasingly capricious and extremely depressed.

It was a year of my life that I'm not proud of.

How and why Donna ever put up with me instead of asking for a divorce I'll never know. I was utterly unbearable – worse still I was aware that I was – and I most assuredly didn't deserve the care and attention she gave me.

But she pulled me through.

After that, as hard as you may find this to believe, there was never another word exchanged in anger between us. There had been more than enough of those during the past year.

Now, you'll recall that when we first met she told me that "The Very Wicked Frog" was both her first and last book. I took that with a pinch of salt at the time, but it proved to be the case. For her, publishing a children's story had been cathartic, something she needed to get out of her system, and with that one book she achieved just that. She never wrote again.

I, on the other hand, had so many stories still to tell.

Donna's unwavering support and encouragement reignited my enthusiasm and six months later we went out for dinner to celebrate the publication of the second Tobias Fulton novel, "A Bullet in the Mist".

I should point out here that I still wasn't making much money, but I was in reasonably good health at that stage, and burying myself in my writing was keeping the Huntington's demons at bay – and by extension, to put it bluntly, saving my marriage.

A year after that "The Snow Killer" was finished. It was in that third Fulton adventure that I decided to have him employ a secretary. And so the fiercely devoted Miss Cavarro was born; call it a very small thank you to my faithful wife.

Donna had been right when she once said that the ignominy of book fairs wasn't for us. We had no place in that world of disillusionment. So at her suggestion we took the bull by the horns and went ahead and created our own little business.

Tobias Fulton became a cottage industry. We were advertising worldwide in select magazines and selling my books from home. Sales were unremarkable, but steady. Life was good.

Then all of a sudden, in the course of a single day, everything changed with the arrival of two letters in the post.

One of them was the result of my latest check-up at the hospital. I had been for so many of them since my diagnosis that I had become a little blasé. I set that aside in favour of the one that looked far more interesting. It was the emblem of the prolific publishing house Hodder & Stoughton on the envelope that had caught my eye.

With trembling fingers I tore it open. I could scarcely believe what I read. Someone in their acquisitions department had stumbled across a copy of "A Bullet in the Mist" and they were very keen to with me at my earliest convenience with a view to publishing it for a wider market. Furthermore, they expressed an interest in seeing "Stolen Midnight" and "The Snow Killer" too.

If you had asked me, I'd have said it was impossible that I could be any happier than I was at that moment.

But then I opened the letter from the hospital.

My latest round of tests had revealed that I was completely free of all evidence of Huntington's disease. I was incredulous. Surely there had to be some sort of mistake. I immediately got on the phone to my consultant, who confirmed what the letter had told me. I was no longer ill. He said that he wanted to carry out some additional tests to be certain, for as far as he was aware nobody who had ever been diagnosed with Huntington's disease had been cured. I kid you not, this was a man of medicine who deals with facts speaking to me and yet he actually called it a miracle.

All my Christmases had come at once and we celebrated in style that night, I don't mind telling you.

I had found my place in this world at last.

It must have been six years later that Donna revealed to me what she had done and how she now feared it had been the most terrible mistake.

What is this thing that builds our dreams, yet slips away from us?

I never liked how I look very much. I always wished I'd had chiselled good looks, but I have one of those unmemorable faces. Not bad-looking as such, but average and... well, forgettable I suppose.

One morning I was standing in the bathroom, examining myself closely in the mirror, something I very seldom did.

I ran a hand through my shock of thick, ebony black hair. 'You know what? I'm 36 years old and I still haven't got a single grey hair on my head.'

Donna stepped out of the shower behind me. 'I know. I wish I was that lucky.' She wrapped a towel around herself.

I turned to look at her. She was two years younger than me, but her beautiful blonde curls were showing small traces of silver. Nevertheless, to me she looked as gorgeous as the day we'd first met. I took her in my arms and looked into those captivating sapphire eyes.

'You haven't got any wrinkles on your face either,' she said. 'Not one.'

I turned back to the mirror. She was right. I hadn't even noticed. In fact, the more I thought about it, I looked barely a day older than I had at the launch event for the initial Tobias Fulton trilogy, which Hodder & Stoughton had hosted at a West End hotel five years earlier.

I went through to the back room that had become my writing retreat and looked at the framed photograph from that evening. It was on the wall above a shelf that contained copies of not only the first three Fulton adventures, but the four that I'd written since: "Secret Fury", "Burning Menace", "Season of Innocence" and – my favourite – "The Broken House".

The photograph of the event showed myself standing between the Managing Director of Hodder's – I forget his name now – and Neville King, one of their

171

top-selling authors at the time, who later committed suicide in the midst of a particularly unsavoury scandal.

I took down the photograph, stepped over to the window where there was more light and examined it closely. I really *hadn't* aged. Not one bit. How had I never realised that before?

Now, nobody likes to see their youthful looks fade. Most people would be delighted to have put the brakes on the ageing process. But it played on my mind inordinately. It just wasn't normal.

I kept on about it all day. I even suggested to Donna that I should maybe see my GP. The memory of the inexplicable exodus of the Huntington's symptoms from my system still mystified me. The medical community had been completely flummoxed. Maybe this was a sign of something else, something rare that the doctors hadn't picked up on.

I was so wrapped up in myself that I failed to notice that Donna was unusually quiet. Even if I had noticed, I'd have probably assumed she was just fed up with me prattling on about something so inconsequential.

That night in bed everything became clear.

I have to pause to ask: Do you believe in wishes coming true? I believe you can wish you had something and, if you want it badly enough, *make* it happen by working hard in the pursuit of it. But in terms of making a spontaneous wish and having it granted by some mystical force? No, I most certainly don't. Blowing out the birthday candles… pulling the wishbone on a chicken carcass… wishing upon a star.

The very idea is twaddle. And at the risk of sounding curmudgeonly, parents who lead their children to believe otherwise are irresponsible.

And yet there was no other rational explanation for what Donna told me as we lay there in bed.

'Do you remember that day we took a walk in Blechnum Woods?'

I had to confess I didn't. I didn't even remember the *name* Blechnum, let alone having been there.

'About six years ago.'

I chuckled. 'I can't remember what we did six weeks ago, let alone six years.'

'It was just before you got the all clear from the hospital. And your book deal.'

I chuckled again. 'Well I'm not likely to forget *that* day, am I? But Blechnum, I can't quite…'

'We stumbled across a wishing well in the woods.'

Of course! I suddenly remembered. I smiled. 'Oh yes, and you said I ought to write a bit in the next Fulton where he finds some bodies in a well, and I said they probably kicked the bucket.'

Donna didn't laugh. She always laughed at my jokes. Even the bad ones.

'What made you think about that?'

'There's something I need to tell you.' There was a discernible tremor in her voice.

I switched on the bedside lamp and turned to face her. She was laid on her back and there were tears in her eyes. 'What's the matter?'

'I did a terrible thing. I mean, it wasn't meant to be terrible, but I think it's turned out that way.'

I was completely confused. I couldn't begin to think what she was talking about.

'Do you remember when we were standing beside the well I said we ought to make a wish, something like your books becoming best-sellers?'

'Not really, no.'

'Well, I did. And you pooh-poohed it. You said that you never get anything for nothing in life and if you want something you have to work hard to get it.'

I laughed. 'That certainly sounds exactly like me. So what?'

'There was an unusual bird in the branches of a tree nearby and you were fascinated by it.'

'Okay.'

'While you were distracted I threw a coin into the well and made a wish.'

To this day I can recall that I rolled my eyes.

'It wasn't for me,' she continued. 'It was for you.'

'What did you wish?'

'It was only for fun. I didn't really think anything would actually happen.'

It was late, I was tired and I wanted to be up and writing early the following morning. I'd had a terrific idea for a twist in the new Fulton I was working on, "The Forever Clause". Yes, I know, the exquisite irony of that title isn't lost on me either, but it was pure coincidence, I assure you. Anyhow, I confess that the conversation was now beginning to irritate me a tad.

174

'Okay,' I said, trying to retain my equanimity. 'But *what* did you wish for?'

A single tear rolled down her cheek and she turned her head to face me. 'I wished that your writing would go on forever.'

I laughed. 'Well what's so terrible about that?'

'I think…' The words seemed to stick in her throat. 'I think something's gone wrong.'

I suspect that you may be ahead of me right now, but I still didn't understand where this was leading.

'It was only about a week later that you got the letter from Hodder's to say they wanted to publish the Fulton books.'

'Okay. But I still don't see what that's got to do with that day in Blechnum. You're not honestly trying to tell me you think that happened because of a frivolous wish?'

'I am.'

I smiled. 'Well, I don't believe it for one moment. But if it really did happen because you wished for it I suppose I should say thank you.'

'But the same day you got the letter saying the Huntington's was gone.'

'I know. But what's that got to do with me being a successful writer?'

'That's not what I wished for.'

I frowned. 'You just said that you did.'

'No, I didn't. I said I wished that your writing would go on forever.'

'What's the difference?'

'This is going to sound crazy, but I think the well misunderstood what I wanted.'

I couldn't help laughing. 'That's preposterous,' I leant over to kiss her, but she pulled away.

'I think I worded it wrong.'

'Honestly, you can't be serious about any of this.'

'But I am.'

'Well then, why didn't you wish for something like... oh, I don't know, my illness to go away?'

'I wasn't thinking about that. It was a spontaneous thing. Even if I'd had time to stop and think about it, I suppose I'd have thought that it wasn't possible for a terminal illness to be cured.'

'But you thought that wishing I was a famous author *could*?'

'You're not listening to me. I wanted your books to live on after you'd gone. They were great. They *are* great. You always said you wished you could leave something behind to prove that you were here. It filled your dreams. You wanted it so badly. And I wanted it for you too. But I asked for your *writing* to go on *forever*.'

'I still don't...' I faltered as the penny dropped. 'Wait a minute. The only way the actual process of writing could go on forever is if I were here doing it.'

Donna nodded. 'I'm *so* sorry.'

'So, that means I'd have to live...'

'Forever.'

I was still confused. The very suggestion was the stuff of fairytales, yet suddenly I felt a sickening knot in my stomach. 'Why exactly have you decided to tell me this now, after all these years?'

'Because today you finally saw what I noticed a long time ago. You aren't getting any older, Michael. You look exactly the same as you did five years ago.'

It won't surprise you to hear that it took me a long time to get to sleep that night. But in the morning common sense returned and I confess I dismissed the whole idea for the fantasy it undoubtedly was. And with some effort I managed to convince Donna too.

Nevertheless, later that week I did go to see my GP, who I must tell you was more than a little bemused by my assertions that I didn't appear to be ageing. Only when I raised concerns about my inexplicable recovery from Huntington's disease did he agree to run some tests.

Aside from a slightly elevated heart rate, everything came back normal.

Only as the weeks turned into months and the months into years did it become obvious that something was very wrong indeed.

But I'm beginning to feel very sleepy now and time is running out. I must finish this story before it's too late.

Here I sit, the celebrated author of 24 full-length Tobias Fulton novels and four short story compendiums, all of them translated into 72 languages around the world. Oh, and don't forget what I anticipate will be the final adventure, "Fulton's Farewell", which is being proofread right now; it's the only time I have used his name in the title, but it felt appropriate for the occasion.

Those books are my legacy and I am certain that they will be read and enjoyed by countless millions for many years to come.

But you know what the strangest thing is? I don't care any more. None of it matters.

Donna Chalvington, who I first met 62 years ago – a woman that I could only ever have dreamed of knowing, let alone marrying and spending such a happy life with – passed away at 5:27 this morning.

I sat at her bedside holding her hand, still as elegantly slender and cool as the day I first touched it, only now the skin was paper-thin and mottled with liver spots. She looked into my eyes and the corners of her mouth curled into that beautiful smile, then I felt my heart break as she slipped quietly away.

She was the love of my life and she's gone.

It wasn't a shock as such. She had been ill for some time. But nothing can ever really prepare you for the death of a loved one, can it?

What you *can* prepare for, is that which comes afterwards.

As I sit here writing this now, I am 87 years old. Yet I do not look a day over 30 and I'm in no doubt that if I lived to be 187 I'd not look any different.

God willing I shall find never out.

Just before I started to write all this down, I injected myself with 10 grams of pentobarbital. Don't question how I procured it. It wasn't easy. Fortunately I have friends in low places.

However, I'm reliably informed that 10 grams is considered to be a lethal dose.

I shall say here that I momentarily feared that injecting myself first would prove a mistake and it might act too quickly for me to be able to tell you my story in as much detail as I wanted.

Fate has at least been kind in that respect, for only in the last few minutes do I feel it has actually started to take effect.

Of course, I realise that the delayed reaction suggests the outcome might not be what I had planned at all.

Will it kill me or will it not?

Obviously I thought it *might* and… well, I had to try. At this moment I honestly have no idea. Yet I imagine it won't be too long before I'll know for sure one way or the other.

All I can say is that I dearly hope I shall be reunited with my beloved Donna again before the night is through. And why should I not be? If a wish made upon a coin tossed frivolously into a well can actually come true, who can honestly claim to know that there's nothing else for us beyond this mortal coil?

And besides, who wants to live forever?

ALL'S WELL THAT ENDS WELL

Rebecca Xibalba

With the sad knowledge that the old brick well in Blechnum Woods was rumoured to be linked to the tragic loss of thirty school children still playing on his mind, Dave left for work in a less than jubilant mood. He wasn't a superstitious man and considered himself to be open minded, but he wasn't easily sucked in by paranormal hearsay and fantasy.

The Meadowbridge estate had been in planning for almost eight years and despite local opposition it had finally been passed and construction was due to start.

Dave had decided not to share the information with his colleagues; it presented no legal implications and wouldn't impact on the infrastructure anyway, so he felt not only was it pointless to raise the issue but would probably be the stimuli for ridicule if he did.

As he approached the site, he could see that following the green light from the local authorities there had been no delay in the preparations.

Dave took his hard hat out of the boot and made his way towards the site office. He pulled the handle and pushed the door but it didn't budge; the portacabin office was locked. He looked around the site and noticed a crowd of people assembled by a large digger on the other side of the field, so he strode over to join them.

'Morning Dave!' one of the men called out as he approached.

The others turned to face him and Dave acknowledged them with a small wave and put his hard hat on. 'Why's the office locked?' he enquired.

'Ollie didn't show up this morning. Apparently there's something wrong with his kid,' one of the men replied.

'Have none of you lot got any keys?'

The men shook their heads in unison.

Dave frowned. 'Okay, well we can crack on, I'll sort the office later.' He handed blueprints out amongst the crowd, and the men scattered and went about their duties.

Dave called out, 'Steve, mate. Can I have a word?'

Steve stopped and walked back towards Dave.

'You're on groundworks aren't you mate?' Dave asked.

'Yeah,' Steve replied.

'Okay, follow me. I need to show you something.'

Dave and Steve strolled off down the hill towards the woodlands.

'What's going on with Ollie?' Dave asked as they walked into the tree line.

'I dunno? His missus called in on Friday. She was a bit cagey, just said their kid wasn't well.'

'Hmm,' Dave replied. 'I hope it's nothing serious. She's a sweet little girl.'

Dave stopped just short of the copse and pulled out a rolled up A3 sheet of paper. 'Right. This is where the main gates will be and up there...' – he pointed – '...will lead to the car parking area.' He pointed to the map. Steve moved in closer to look. 'As you can see, we have a water source here' Dave continued.

'Will that be a problem?' Steve asked.

'No, not at all. Follow me.'

Dave and Steve entered the copse.

'It's just a well,' Dave said. 'No preservation order and the water is probably all but dried up now so it won't affect our work.'

Steve approached the well. 'How old is it?' he asked.

'Fifteen hundreds,' Dave replied.

Steve walked around it. 'Bloody good masonry for something 600 years old,' he quipped.

'Yeah s'pose it is,' Dave agreed.

Steve picked up the wooden sign 'Ha, look. Make a wish! Shall we?' He foraged in his pocket for a coin.

'No!' Dave yelled.

Steve was taken aback.

Dave chuckled nervously. 'We haven't got time to piss about. Besides, I know what you'd wish for and I don't think big breasted women come out of fifteenth century wells!'

'So what's the crack then, boss?' Steve asked. 'Are we going to flatten it?'

'Yep. Fill it in and get it demolished.'

Dave started to walk away.

Steve looked back at the well before following his boss. 'Shame,' he said as they walked away.

Acknowledgements:
The authors would like to thank John Sinclaire-Thomas
for the illustrations throughout.

Cover photography and design by Rebecca Xibalba.

Also from Rebecca Xibalba and Tim Greaves:
Misdial (2020)
The Break (2021)
Available from Amazon, for Kindle and in Paperback.
Misdial is also available in Audiobook format from Audible and iTunes.

Coming Soon:
Reset (2022)

Be careful what you wish for...

Printed in Great Britain
by Amazon